AF147796

Hiram The Young Farmer

by

Burbank L. Todd

Double9
BOOKS

Hiram The Young Farmer
by Burbank L. Todd

Copyright © 2024

All Rights reserved.

No part of this publication may be reproduced,
stored in a retrieval system, or transmitted in any
form or by any means, electronic, mechanical,
photocopying or Otherwise, without the written
permission of the publisher.
The author/editor asserts the moral right to
be identified as the author/editor of this work.

ISBN: 978-93-62203-91-5

Published by

DOUBLE 9 BOOKS

2/13-B, Ansari Road
Daryaganj, New Delhi – 110002
info@double9books.com
www.double9books.com
Tel. 011-40042856

This book is under public domain

ABOUT THE AUTHOR

Burbank L. Todd, a prolific American author, carved his legacy with the timeless classic "Hiram the Young Farmer." Set against the rustic backdrop of rural America, Todd's masterpiece follows the journey of Hiram, a young and determined farmer, as he navigates the challenges of agricultural life and endeavors to carve out his place in the world. Through vivid storytelling and rich character development, Todd paints a compelling portrait of Hiram's trials and triumphs, capturing the essence of hard work, perseverance, and the indomitable spirit of the American dream. With keen insight and a keen eye for detail, Todd expertly weaves together themes of ambition, resilience, and the pursuit of one's passions, making "Hiram the Young Farmer" a timeless classic that resonates with readers of all ages. Todd's work not only celebrates the agricultural heritage of America but also serves as an enduring testament to the human spirit's capacity for growth, adaptation, and triumph in the face of adversity.

CONTENTS

CHAPTER I
THE CALL OF SPRING

"Well, after all, the country isn't such a bad place as some city folk think."

The young fellow who said this stood upon the highest point of the Ridge Road, where the land sloped abruptly to the valley in which lay the small municipality of Crawberry on the one hand, while on the other open fields and patches of woodland, in a huge green-and-brown checkerboard pattern, fell more easily to the bank of the distant river.

Dotted here and there about the farming country lying before the youth as he looked westward were cottages, or the more important-looking homesteads on the larger farms; and in the distance a white church spire behind the trees marked the tiny settlement of Blaine's Smithy.

A Sabbath calm lay over the fields and woods. It was mid-afternoon of an early February Sunday—the time of the mid-winter thaw, that false prophet of the real springtime.

Although not a furrow had been turned as yet in the fields, and the snow lay deep in some fence corners and beneath the hedges, there was, after all, a smell of fresh earth—a clean, live smell—that Hiram Strong had missed all week down in Crawberry.

"I'm glad I came up here," he muttered, drawing in great breaths of the clean air. "Just to look at the open fields, without any brick and mortar around, makes a fellow feel fine!"

He stretched his arms above his head and, standing alone there on the upland, felt bigger and better than he had in weeks.

For Hiram Strong was a country boy, born and bred, and the town stifled him. Besides, he had begun to see that his two years in Crawberry had been wasted.

"As a hustler after fortune in the city I am not a howling success," mused Hiram. "Somehow, I'm cramped down yonder," and he glanced back at the squalid brick houses below him, the smoky roofs, and the ugly factory chimneys.

"And I declare," he pursued, reflectively, "I don't believe I can stand Old Dan Dwight much longer. Dan, Junior, is bad enough—when he is around the store; but the boss would drive a fellow to death."

He shook his head, now turning from the pleasanter prospect of the farming land and staring down into the town.

"Maybe I'm not a success because I don't stick to one thing. I've had six jobs in less'n two years. That's a bad record for a boy, I believe. But there hasn't any of them suited me, nor have I suited them.

"And Dwight's Emporium beats 'em all!" finished Hiram, shaking his head.

He turned his back upon the town once more, as though to wipe his failure out of his memory. Before him sloped a field of wheat and clover.

It had kept as green under the snow as though winter was an unknown season. Every cloverleaf sparkled and the leaves of wheat bristled like tiny spears.

Spring was on the way. He could hear the call of it!

Two years before Hiram had left the farm. He had no immediate relatives after his father died. The latter had been a tenant-farmer only, and when his tools and stock and the few household chattels had been sold to pay the debts that had accumulated during his last illness, there was very little money left for Hiram.

There was nobody to say him nay when he packed his bag and started for Crawberry, which was the metropolis of his part of the country. He had set out boldly, believing that he could get ahead faster, and become master of his own fortune more quickly in town than in the locality where he was born.

He was a rugged, well-set-up youth of seventeen, not over-tall, but sturdy and able to do a man's work. Indeed, he had long done a man's work before he left the farm.

Hiram's hands were calloused, he shuffled a bit when walked, and his shoulders were just a little bowed from holding the plow handles since he had been big enough to bridle his father's old mare.

Yes, the work on the farm had been hard—especially for a growing boy. Many farm boys work under better conditions than Hiram had.

Nevertheless, after a two years' trial of what the city has in store for most country boys who cut loose from their old environment, Hiram Strong felt to-day as though he must get back to the land.

"There's nothing for me in town. Clerking in Dwight's Emporium will never get me anywhere," he thought, turning finally away from the open country and starting down the steep hill.

"Why, there are college boys working on our street cars here—waiting for some better job to turn up. What chance does a fellow stand who's only got a country school education?

"And there isn't any clean fun for a fellow in Crawberry—fun that doesn't cost money. And goodness knows I can't make more than enough to pay Mrs. Atterson, and for my laundry, and buy a new suit of overalls and a pair of shoes occasionally.

"No, sir!" concluded Hiram. "There's nothing in it. Not for a fellow like me, at any rate. I'd better be back on the farm—and I wish I was there now."

He had been to church that morning; but after the late dinner at his boarding house had set out on this lonely walk. Now he had nothing to look forward to as he returned but the stuffy parlor of Mrs. Atterson's boarding house, the cold supper in the dining-room, which was attended in a desultory fashion by such of the boarders as were at home, and then a long, dull evening in his room, or bed after attending the evening service at the church around the corner.

Hiram even shrank from meeting the same faces at the boarding house table, hearing the same stale jokes or caustic remarks about Mrs. Atterson's food from Fred Crackit and the young men boarders of his class, or the grumbling of Mr. Peebles, the dyspeptic invalid, or the inane monologue of Old Lem Camp.

And Mrs. Atterson herself—good soul though she was—had gotten on Hiram Strong's nerves, too. With her heat-blistered face, near-sighted eyes peering through beclouded spectacles, and her gown buttoned up hurriedly and with a gap here and there where a button was missing, she was the typically frowsy, hurried, nagged-to-death boarding house mistress.

And as for "Sister," Mrs. Atterson's little slavey and maid-of-all-work——

"Well, Sister's the limit!" smiled Hiram, as he turned into the street, with its rows of ugly brick houses on either hand. "I believe Fred Crackit has got it right. Mrs. Atterson keeps Sister instead of a cat—so there'll be something to kick."

The half-grown girl—narrow-chested, round shouldered, and sallow— had been taken by Mrs. Atterson from some charity institution. "Sister," as the boarders all called her, for lack of any other cognomen, would have her yellow hair in four attenuated pigtails hanging down her back, and she would shuffle about the dining-room in a pair of Mrs. Atterson's old shoes——

"By Jove! there she is now," exclaimed the startled youth.

At the corner of the street several "slices" of the brick block had been torn away and the lot cleared for the erection of some business building. Running across this open space with wild shrieks and spilling the milk from the big pitcher she carried—milk for the boarders' tea, Hi knew—came Mrs. Atterson's maid.

Behind her, and driving her like a horse by the ever present "pigtails," bounded a boy of about her own age—a laughing, yelling imp of a boy whom Hiram knew very well.

"That Dan Dwight is the meanest little scamp at this end of the town!" he said to himself.

The noise the two made attracted only the idle curiosity of a few people. It was a locality where, even on Sundays, there was more or less noise.

Sister begged and screamed. She feared she would spill the milk and told Dan, Junior, so. But he only drove her the harder, yelling to her to "Get up!" and yanking as hard as he could on the braids.

"Here! that's enough of that!" called Hiram, stepping quickly toward the two.

For Sister had stopped exhausted, and in tears.

"Be off with you!" commanded Hiram. "You've plagued the girl enough."

"Mind your business, Hi-ram-Lo-ram!" returned Dan, Junior, grabbing at Sister's hair again.

Hiram caught the younger boy by the shoulder and whirled him around.

"You run along to Mrs. Atterson, Sister," he said, quietly. "No, you don't!" he added, gripping Dan, Junior, more firmly. "You'll stop right here."

"Lemme be, Hi Strong!" bawled the other, when he found he could not easily jerk away. "It'll be the worse for you if you don't."

"Just you wait until the girl is home," returned Hiram, laughing. It was an easy matter for him to hold the writhing Dan, Junior.

"I'll fix you for this!" squalled the boy. "Wait till I tell my father."

"You wouldn't dare tell your father the truth," laughed Hi.

"I'll fix you," repeated Dan, Junior, and suddenly aimed a vicious kick at his captor.

Had the kick landed where Dan, Junior, intended—under Hi's kneecap—the latter certainly would have been "fixed." But the country youth was too agile for him.

He jumped aside, dragged Dan, Junior, suddenly toward him, and then gave him a backward thrust which sent the lighter boy spinning.

Now, it had rained the day before and in a hollow beside the path was a puddle several inches deep. Dan, Junior, lost his balance, staggered back, tripped over his own clumsy heels, and splashed full length into it.

"Oh, oh!" he bawled, managing to get well soaked before he scrambled out. "I'll tell my father on you, Hi Strong. You'll catch it for this!"

"You'd better run home before you catch cold," said Hiram, who could not help laughing at the young rascal's plight. "And let girls alone another time."

To himself he said: "Well, the goodness knows I couldn't be much more in bad odor with Mr. Dwight than I am already. But this escapade of his precious son ought to about 'fix' me, as Dan, Junior, says.

"Whether I want to, or not, I reckon I will be looking for another job in a very few days."

CHAPTER II
AT MRS. ATTERSON'S

When you came into "Mother" Atterson's front hall (the young men boarders gave her that appellation in irony) the ghosts of many ancient boiled dinners met you with—if you were sensitive and unused to the odors of cheap boarding houses—a certain shock.

He was starting up the stairs, on which the ragged carpet threatened to send less agile persons than Mrs. Atterson's boarders headlong to the bottom at every downward trip, when the clang of the gong in the dining-room announced the usual cold spread which the landlady thought due to her household on the first day of the week.

Hiram hesitated, decided that he would skip the meal, and started up again. But just then Fred Crackit lounged out of the parlor, with Mr. Peebles following him. Dyspeptic as he was, Mr. Peebles never missed a meal himself, and Crackit said:

"Come on, Hi-Low-Jack! Aren't you coming down to the usual feast of reason and flow of soul?"

Crackit thought he was a natural humorist, and he had to keep up his reputation at all times and seasons. He was rather a dissipated-looking man of thirty years or so, given to gay waistcoats and wonderfully knit ties. A brilliant as large as a hazel-nut—and which, in some lights, really sparkled like a diamond—adorned the tie he wore this evening.

"I don't believe I want any supper," responded Hiram, pleasantly.

"What's the matter? Got some inside information as to what Mother Atterson has laid out for us? You're pretty thick with the old girl, Hi."

"That's not a nice way to speak of her, Mr. Crackit," said Hi, in a low voice.

The other boarders—those who were in the house-straggled into the basement dining-room one after the other, and took their places at the long table, each in his customary manner.

That dining-room at Mother Atterson's never could have been a cheerful place. It was long, and low-ceiled, and the paper on the walls was a dingy red, so old that the figure on it had retired into the background—been absorbed by it, so to speak.

The two long, dusty, windows looked upon an area, and were grilled half way up by wrought-iron screens which, too, helped to shut out the light of day.

The long table was covered by a red figured table cloth. The "castors" at both ends and in the middle were the ugliest—Hiram was sure—to be found in all the city of Crawberry. The crockery was of the coarsest kind. The knives and forks were antediluvian. The napkins were as coarse as huck towels.

But Mrs. Atterson's food—considering the cost of provisions and the charge she made for her table—was very good. Only it had become a habit for certain of the boarders, led by the jester, Crackit, to criticise the viands.

Sometimes they succeeded in making Mrs. Atterson angry; and sometimes, Hiram knew, she wept, alone in the dining-room, after the harumscarum, thoughtless crowd had gone.

Old Lem Camp—nobody save Hiram thought to put "Mr." before the old gentleman's name—sidled in and sat down beside the country boy, as usual. He was a queer, colorless sort of person—a man who never looked into the face of another if he could help it. He would look all around Hiram when he spoke to him—at his shoulder, his shirtfront, his hands, even at his feet if they were visible, but never at his face.

And at the table he kept up a continual monologue. It was difficult sometimes for Hiram to know when he was being addressed, and when poor Mr. Camp was merely talking to himself.

"Let's see—where has Sister put my napkin—Oh! here it is—You've been for a walk, have you, young man?—No, that's not my napkin; I didn't spill any gravy at dinner—Nice day out, but raw—Goodness me! can't I have a knife and fork?—Where's my knife and fork?—Sister certainly has forgotten my knife and fork.—Oh! Here they are—Yes, a very nice day indeed for this time of year."

And so on. It was quite immaterial to Mr. Camp whether he got an answer to his remarks to Hiram, or not. He went on muttering to himself, all through the meal, sometimes commenting upon what the others said at the table—and that quite shrewdly, Hiram noticed; but the other boarders considered him a little cracked.

Sister smiled sheepishly at Hiram as she passed the tea. She drowned his tea with milk and put in no less than four spoonfuls of sugar. But although the fluid was utterly spoiled for Hiram's taste he drank it with fortitude, knowing that the girl's generosity was the child of her gratitude; for both sugar and milk were articles very scantily supplied at Mother Atterson's table.

The mistress herself did not appear. Now that he was down here in the dining-room, Hiram lingered. He hated the thought of going up to his lonely and narrow quarters at the top of the house.

The other boarders trailed out of the room and up stairs, one after another, Old Lem Camp being the last to go. Sister brought in a dish of hot toast between two plates and set it at the upper end of the table. Then Mrs. Atterson appeared.

Hiram knew at once that something had gone wrong with the boarding house mistress. She had been crying, and when a woman of the age of Mrs. Atterson indulges in tears, her personal appearance is never improved.

"Oh, that you, Hi?" she drawled, with a snuffle. "Did you get enough to eat?"

"Yes, Mrs. Atterson," returned the youth, starting to get up. "I have had plenty."

"I'm glad you did," said the lady. "And you're easy 'side of most of 'em, Hiram. You're a real good boy."

"I reckon I get all I pay for, Mrs. Atterson," said her youngest boarder.

"Well, there ain't many of 'em would say that. And they was awful provokin' this noon. That roast of veal was just as good meat as I could find in market; and I don't know what any sensible party would want better than that prune pie.

"Well! I hope I won't have to keep a boarding house all my life. It's a thankless task. An' it ties a body down so.

"Here's my uncle—my poor mother's only brother and about the only relative I've got in the world—here's Uncle Jeptha down with the grip, or suthin', and goodness knows if he'll ever get over it. And I can't leave to go and see him die peaceable."

"Does he live far from here?" asked Hiram, politely, although he had no particular reason for being interested in Uncle Jeptha.

"He lives on a farm out Scoville way. He's lived there most all his life. He used to make a right good living off'n that farm, too; but it's run down some now.

"The last time I was out there, two years ago, he was just keepin' along and that's all. And now I expect he's dying, without a chick or child of his own by him," and she burst out crying again, the tears sprinkling the square of toast into which she continued to bite.

Of course, it was ridiculous. A middle-aged woman weeping and eating toast and drinking strong boiled tea is not a romantic picture. But as Hiram climbed to his room he wished with all his heart that he could help Mrs. Atterson.

He wasn't the only person in the world who seemed to have got into a wrong environment—lots of people didn't fit right into their circumstances in life.

"We're square pegs in round holes—that's what we are," mused Hiram. "That's what I am. I wish I was out of it. I wish I was back on the farm."

CHAPTER III
A DREARY DAY

Daniel Dwight's Emporium, the general store was called, and it was in a very populous part of the town of Crawberry. Old Daniel was a driver, he seldom had clerks enough to handle his trade properly, and nobody could suit him. As general helper and junior clerk, Hiram Strong had remained with the concern longer than any other boy Daniel had hired in years.

When the early Monday morning rush was over, and there was moment's breathing space, Hiram went to the door to re-arrange the trays of vegetables which were his particular care. Hiram had a knack of making a bank of the most plebeian vegetable and salads look like the display-window of a florist.

Now the youth looked out upon a typical city street, the dwellings on either side being four and five story tenement houses, occupied by artisans and mechanics.

A few quarreling children paddled sticks, or sailed chip boats, in the gutters.

"Come on, now! Get a move on you, Hi!" sounded the raucous voice of Daniel Dwight the elder, behind him in the store.

Hiram went at his task with neither interest nor energy.

All about him the houses and the street were grimy and depressing. It had been a gray and murky morning; but overhead a patch of sky was as blue as June. He suddenly saw a flock of pigeons wheeling above the tunnel of the street, and the boy's heart leaped at the sight.

He longed for freedom. He wished he could fly, up, up, up above the housetops and the streets, like those feathered fowl.

He knew he was stagnating here in this dingy store; the deadly sameness of his life chafed him sorely.

"I'd take another job if I could find one," he muttered, stirring up the bunches of yellowing radish leaves and trying to make them look fresh. "And Old Daniel is likely to give me a chance to hunt a job pretty sudden—

the way he talks. But if Dan, Junior, told him what happened yesterday, I wonder the old gentleman hasn't been after me with a sharp stick."

From somewhere—out of the far-distant open country where it had been breathing all night the quivering pines, and brown swamps, and the white and gray checkered fields that would soon be upturned by the plowshares—a vagrant wind wandered into the city street.

The lingering, but faint perfume wafted here from God's open world to die in this man-made town inspired in the youth thoughts and desires that had been struggling within him for expression for days past.

"I know what I want," said Hiram Strong, aloud. "I want to get back to the land!"

The progress of the day was not inducive to a hopeful outlook for Hiram. When closing time came he was heartily sick of the business of storekeeping, if he never had been before.

And when he dragged himself home to the boarding house, he found the atmosphere there as dreary as the street itself. The boarders were grumpy and Mrs. Atterson was in a tearful state again.

Hiram could not stay in his room. It was a narrow, cold place at the end of the back hall at the top of the house. There was a little, painted bureau in it, one leg of which had been replaced by a brick, and the little glass was so blue and blurred that he never could see in it whether his tie was straight or not.

There was a chair, a shelf for books, and a narrow folding bed. When the bed was dropped down for his occupancy at night, he could not get the door open. Had there ever been a fire at Atterson's at night, Hiram's best chance for escape would have been by the window.

So this evening, to kill the miserable stretch of time until sleep should come to him, the boy went out and walked the streets.

Two things had saved Hiram Strong from getting into bad company on these evening rambles. One was the small amount of money he earned, and the other was the naturally clean nature of the boy. The cheap amusements which lured on either hand did not attract him.

But the dangers are there in every city, and they lurk for every boy in a like position.

The main thoroughfare in this part of the town where Hiram boarded was brightly lighted, gaudy electric signs attracting notice to cheap picture shows, catch-penny arcades, cheap jewelry stores, and the ever present saloons and pool rooms.

It looked bright, and warm, and lively in many of these places; but the country-bred boy was cautious.

Now and then a raucous-voiced automobile shot along the street; the electric cars made their usual clangor, and there was still some ordinary traffic of the day dribbling away into the side streets, for it was early in the evening.

Hiram was about to turn into one of these side streets on his way back to Mrs. Atterson's. Turning the corner was a handsome span of horses attached to a comfortable but mud-bespattered carriage. It was plainly from the country.

The light at the corner of the street shone brightly into the carriage. Hiram saw a well-built man in a gray greatcoat and slouch hat, holding the reins over the backs of the spirited horses.

Beside him sat a girl. She could have been no more than twelve or fourteen—not so old as Sister, by a year or two. But how different she was from the starved-looking, boarding house slavey!

She was framed in furs—rich, gray and black furs that muffled her from top to toe, only leaving her brilliant, dark little face with its perfect features shining like a jewel in its setting.

She was talking laughingly to the big man beside her, and he was looking down at her. Perhaps this was why he did not see what lay just ahead—or perhaps the glare of the street light blinded him, as it must have the horses, as the equipage turned into the darker side street.

But Hiram saw their peril. He sprang into the street with a cry of warning. And he was lucky enough to seize the nigh horse by the bridle and pull both the high-steppers around.

There was an excavation—an opening for a water-main—in this street. The workmen had either neglected to leave a red lantern, or malicious boys had stolen it.

Another moment and the horses would have been in this excavation and even now the carriage swayed. One forward wheel went over the edge of the hole, and for the minute it was doubtful whether Hiram had saved the occupants of the carriage by his quick action, or had accelerated the catastrophe.

CHAPTER IV
THE LOST CARD

Had Hiram Strong not been a muscular youth for his age, and sturdy withal, the excited horses would have broken away from him and the carriage would certainly have gone into the ditch.

But he had a grip on the bridle reins now that could not be broken, although the horses plunged and struck fire from the stones of the street with their shoes. He dragged them forward, the carriage pitched and rolled for a moment, and then stood upright again, squarely on its four wheels.

"All right, lad! I've got 'em!" exclaimed the gentleman in the carriage.

He had a hearty, husky sort of voice—a voice that came from deep down in his chest and was more than a little hoarse. But there was no quiver of excitement in it. Indeed, he who had been in peril was much less disturbed by the incident than was Hiram himself.

Nor had the girl screamed, or otherwise voiced her terror. Now Hiram heard her say, as he stepped back from the plunging horses:

"That is a good boy, Daddy. Speak to him again."

The man in gray laughed. He was now holding in the frightened team with one firm hand while he fumbled in the pocket of his big coat with the other.

"He certainly has got some muscle, that lad," announced the gentleman. "Here, son, where can I find you when I'm in town again?"

"I work at Dwight's Emporium," replied Hiram, rather diffidently.

"All right. Thanks. Here's my card. You're the kind of a boy I like. I'll surely look you up."

He held out the bit of pasteboard to Hiram; but as the youth stepped nearer to reach it, the impatient horses sprang forward and the carriage rolled swiftly by him.

The card flipped from the man's fingers. Hiram grabbed for it, but missed the card. It fluttered into the excavation in the street and the shadow hid it completely from the boy's gaze.

Had there been a lantern nearby, as there should have been, Hiram would have taken it to search for the lost card. For he felt suddenly as though Opportunity had brushed past him.

The man in the carriage evidently lived out of town. He might be a prosperous farmer. And, being a farmer, he might be able to give Hiram just the sort of job he was looking for.

The card, of course, would have put Hiram in touch with the man. And he seemed like a hearty, good-natured individual.

"And the girl—his daughter—was as pretty as a picture," thought Hiram, as he turned wearily toward the boarding house. "Well! I don't know that I'll ever see either of them again; but if I could learn that man's name and address I'd certainly look him up."

So much did this thought disturb him that he was up an hour earlier than usual the next morning and hurried to work by the way of the excavation in the street where the incident had occurred.

But he could not find the card, although he got down into the ditch to search for it. The loose sand, perhaps, rattling down from the sides of the excavation during the night, had buried the bit of pasteboard, and Hiram went on to Dwight's Emporium more disheartened than ever.

The work there went worse that morning. Old Daniel Dwight drove the young fellow from one task to another. The other clerks got a minute's time to themselves now and then; but the proprietor of the store seemed to have his keen eyes on Hiram continually.

There was always a slow-up in the work about ten o'clock, and Hiram had a request to make. He asked Old Daniel for an hour off.

"An hour off—with all this work to do? What do you mean, boy?" roared the proprietor. "What do you want an hour for?"

"I've got an errand," replied Hiram, quietly.

"Well, what is it?" snarled the old man, curiously.

"Why—it's a private matter. I can't tell you," returned the youth, coolly.

"No good, I'll be bound—no good. I don't see why I should let you off an hour——"

"I work many an hour overtime for you, Mr. Dwight," put in Hiram.

"Yes, yes; that's all right. That's the agreement. You knew you'd have to when you came to work at the Emporium. Stick to your contract, boy."

"Then why don't you stick to yours?" demanded the youth, boldly.

"Eh! Eh! What do you mean by that?" cried Mr. Dwight, glaring at Hiram through his spectacles.

"I mean that when I came to work for you seven months ago, you promised that, if I suited after six months, you would raise my wages. And you haven't done so," said the young fellow, firmly.

For a moment the proprietor of the Emporium was dumb. It was true. He had promised just that. He had got the boy cheaper by so doing. But never before had he hired a boy who stayed as long as six months, so he had never had to raise his wages.

"Well, well!"

He stammered for a moment; then a shrewd thought came to his mind. He actually smiled. When Mr. Dwight smiled it was worse than when he didn't.

"I told you that if you suited me I'd raise your pay, did I?" he snarled. "Well, you don't suit me. You never have suited me. Therefore, you get no raise, young man."

Hiram was not astonished; he was only indignant. Another boy might have expressed his anger by flaring up and tendering his resignation on the spot.

But Hiram had that fear of debt in his breast which is almost always a characteristic of the frugal, country-bred person. He had saved little. He had no prospect of another job. And every Saturday night he was expected to pay Mrs. Atterson three dollars and a half.

"At any rate, Mr. Dwight," he said, quietly, after a minute's silence, "I want an hour to myself this morning."

"And I'll dock ye ten cents for it," declared the old man.

"You can do as you like about that," returned Hiram, and he walked into the back room, took off his apron, and got into his coat.

He had it in mind to go to the big market, where the farmers drove in from out of town, and see if he could meet one of his old neighbors, or anybody else who could tell him of prospect of work for the coming season. It was early yet for farmers to be looking for extra hands; but Hiram hoped that he might see something in prospect for the future. He had made up his mind that, if possible, he would not take another job in town.

"And I can see pretty plainly that I've got about through at the Emporium," he thought, as he approached the open space devoted by the City of Crawberry to a market for the truckmen and farmers who drove in with their wares from the surrounding country.

At this time of day the bustle of market was over. The farmers would have had their breakfasts in the little restaurants which encircled the market-place, or would be preparing to drive home again. The hucksters and push-cart merchants were picking up "seconds" and lot-ends of vegetables for their trade. The cobbles of the market-place was a litter of cabbage leaves, spilled sprouts, spoiled potatoes, and other refuse.

Hiram walked about, looking for somebody whom he knew; but most of the faces around the market were strange to him. Several farmers he spoke to about work; but they were not hiring hands, so, when his hour was up, he went back to the Emporium, more despondent than before.

CHAPTER V
THE COMMOTION AT MOTHER ATTERSON'S

By chance that evening Hiram got home to his boarding house in good season. The early boarders—"early birds" Crackit always termed them—had not yet sat down to the long table in the dingy dining-room.

Indeed, the supper gong had not been pounded by Sister, and some of the young men were grouped impatiently in the half-lighted parlor.

Through the swinging door into the steaming kitchen Hiram saw a huge black woman waddling about the range, and heard her husky voice berating Sister for not moving faster. Chloe only appeared when a catastrophe happened at the boarding-house—and a catastrophe meant the removal of Mrs. Atterson from her usual orbit.

"She's gone to the funeral. That Uncle Jeptha of hern is dead," whispered Sister in Hiram's ear when she put his soup in front of him.

"Ah-ha!" observed Mr. Crackit, eyeing Hiram with his head on one side, "secrets, eh? Inside information of what's in the pudding sauce?"

Nothing went right at the boarding-house during the next two days. And for Hiram Strong nothing seemed to go right anywhere!

He demanded—and got the permission, with another ten-cent tax—another hour off to visit the market. But he found nobody who would hire a boy at once. Some of the farmers doubted if he knew as much about farm-work as he claimed to know. He was, after all, a boy, and some of them would not believe that he had even worked in the country.

Affairs at the Emporium were getting strained, too. Daniel Dwight was as shrewd a man as the next one. He saw plainly that his junior clerk was getting ready—like the many who had gone before him—for a flitting.

He knew the signs of discontent, although Hiram prided himself on doing his work just as well as ever.

Then, there was a squabble with Dan, Junior. The imp was always underfoot on Saturdays. He was supposed to help—to run errands, and take out in a basket certain orders to nearby customers who might be in a hurry.

But usually when you wanted the boy he was in the alley pitching buttons with loafing urchins of his own kind—"alley rats" his father angrily called them—or leading a predatory gang of the same unsavory companions in raids on other stores in the neighborhood.

And Dan, Junior "had it in" for Hiram. He had not forgiven the bigger boy for pitching him into the puddle.

"An' them was my best clo'es, and now maw says I've got to wear 'em just the same on Sunday, and they're shrunk and stained," snarled the younger Dan, hovering about Hiram as the latter re-dressed the fruit stand during a moment's let-up in the Saturday morning rush. "Gimme an orange."

"What! At five cents apiece?" exclaimed Hiram. "Guess not. Go look in the basket under the bench; maybe there's a specked one there."

"Nope. Dad took 'em all home last night and maw cut out the specks and sliced 'em for supper. Gimme a good orange."

"Ask your father," said Hiram.

"Naw, I won't!" declared young Dwight, knowing very well what his father's answer would be.

He suddenly made a grab for the golden globe on the apex of Hiram's handsomest pyramid.

"Let that alone, Dan!" cried Hiram, and seized the youngster by the wrist.

Dan, Junior, was a wiry little scamp, and he twisted and turned, and kicked and squalled, and Hiram was just wrenching the orange from his hand when Mr. Dwight came to the door.

"What's this? What's this?" he demanded. "Fighting, are ye? Why don't you tackle a fellow of your own size, Hi Strong?"

At that Dan, Junior, saw his chance and broke into woeful sobs. He was a good actor.

"I've a mind to turn you over to a policeman, Hiram," cried "Mr. Dwight, That's what I've a mind to do."

"I suppose you'll discharge me first, won't you?" suggested Hiram, scornfully.

"You can come in and git your money right now, young man," said the proprietor of the Emporium. "Dan! let them oranges alone. And don't you go away from here. I'll want you all day to-day. I shall be short-handed with this young scalawag leaving me in the lurch like this."

It had come so suddenly that Hiram almost lost his breath. He had part of his wish, that was sure. He was not likely to work for Daniel Dwight any longer.

The old man led the way back to his office. He had a little pile of money already counted out upon the desk. It was plain that he had intended quarreling with Hiram and getting rid of him at this time, for he had the young fellow's wages figured up to t hat very hour—and twenty cents deducted for the two hours Hiram had had "off."

"But that isn't fair. I'm willing to work to the end of the day. I ought to get my wages in full for the week, save for the twenty cents," said Hiram mildly.

To tell the truth, now that he had lost his job—unpleasant as it had been—Hiram was more than a little troubled. He was indeed about to be cast adrift.

"You'll git jest that sum, and not a cent more," declared Mr. Dwight, sharply. "And if you start any trouble here I'll call in the officer on the beat—yes, I will! I don't know but I ought to deduct the cost of Dan, Junior's, spoiled suit, too. He says you an' he was skylarkin' on Sunday and that's how he fell into the water."

Hiram had no answer to make to this. What was the use? He took the money, slipped it into his pocket, and went out.

He did not linger around the Emporium. Nor was he scarcely out of sight when a man driving a span of handsome bay horses halted his team before the store, jumped out, and went in.

"Are you the proprietor of Dwight's Emporium?" asked the man in the gray coat and hat, in his hearty tones. "You are? Glad to meet you! I'm looking for a young man who works for you."

"Who's that? What do you want of him?" asked Dan, Senior, doubtfully, and rubbing his hand, for the stranger's grip had been as hearty as his voice.

The other laughed in his jovial way. "Why, to tell the truth, I don't know his name. I didn't ask him. He's not much more than a boy—a sturdy youngster with a quick way with him. He did me a service the other evening and I wanted to see him."

"There ain't any boy working here," snapped Mr. Dwight. "Them's all the clerks I got behind the counter—and there ain't one of 'em under thirty, I'll be bound."

"That's so," admitted the stranger. "And although it was so dark I could not see that fellow's face, and I didn't ask his name, I am sure he was young."

"I jest discharged the only boy I had—and scamp enough he was," snarled Mr. Dwight. "If you were looking for him, you'd have been sorry to find him. I didn't know but I'd have to send for a policeman to git him off the premises."

"What—what?"

"That's what I tell you. He was a bad egg. Mebbe he's the boy you want—but you won't get no good of him when you find him. And I've no idea where he's to be found now," and the old man turned his back on the man in the gray coat and went into his office.

The stranger climbed back into his buggy and took up the lines again with a preoccupied headshake.

"Now, I promised Lettie," he muttered, "that I'd find out all about that boy—and maybe bring him home with me. Funny that man gave his such a bad character. Wish I could have seen the lad's face the other night—that would have told the story.

"Well," and he dismissed the matter with a sigh, for he was busy man, "if he's got my card, and he is out of a job, perhaps he'll look me up. Then we'll see."

CHAPTER VI
THIS DIDN'T GET BY HIRAM

"I've sure got plenty of time now to look for a job," observed Hiram Strong when he was two blocks away from Dwight's Emporium. "But I declare I don't know where to begin."

For his experience in talking with the farmers around the market had rather dashed Hiram's hope of getting a place in the country at once. It was too early in the season. Nor did it look so much like Spring as it had a week ago. Already Hiram had to turn up the collar of his rough coat, and a few flakes of snow were settling on his shoulders as he walked.

"It's winter yet," he mused. "If I can't get something to do in the city for a few weeks to tide me over, I'm afraid I shall have to find a cheaper place to board than at Mother Atterson's."

After half an hour of strolling from street to street, however, Hiram decided that there was nothing in that game. He must break in somewhere, so he turned into the very next warehouse.

"Want a job? I'll be looking for one myself pretty soon, if business isn't better," was the answer he got from the first man he approached.

But Hiram kept at it, and got short answers and long answers, pleasant ones and some that were not so pleasant; but all could be summed up in the single monosyllable:

"No!"

"I certainly am a failure here in town," Hiram thought, as he walked through the snow-blown streets. "How foolish I was ever to have come away from the country.

"A fellow ought to stick to the job he is fitted for—and that's sure. But I didn't know. I thought there would be forty chances in town to one in the country.

"And there doesn't seem to be a single chance right now. Why, I'll have to leave Mrs. Atterson's, if I can't find a job before next week is out!

"This mean old town is over-crowded with fellows like me looking for work. And when it comes to office positions, I haven't a high-school diploma, nor am I fitted for that kind of a job.

"I want to be out of doors. Working in a stuffy office wouldn't suit me. Oh, as a worker in the city I am a rank failure, and that's all there is about it!"

He went home to supper much more tired than he would have been had he done a full day's work at Dwight's Emporium. Indeed, the job he had lost now loomed up in his troubled mind as much more important than it had seemed when he had desired to change it for another.

Mother Atterson was at home. She hadn't more than taken off her bonnet, however, and had had but a single clash with Chloe in the kitchen.

"I smelled it burnin' the minute I set my foot on the front step!" she declared. "You can't fool my nose when it comes to smelling burned stuff.

"Well, Hiram," she continued, too full of news to remark that he was at home long before his time, "I saw the poor old soul laid away, at least. I wish now I'd got Chloe in before, and gone to see Uncle Jeptha before he was in his coffin.

"But I didn't think I could afford it, and that's a fact. We poor folks can't have many pleasures in this world of toil and trouble!" added the boarding house mistress, to whom even the break of a funeral, or a death-bed visit, was in the nature of a solemn amusement.

"And there the old man went and made his will years ago, unbeknownst to anybody, and me bein' his only blood relation, as you might say, though it was years since I seen him much, but he remembered my mother with love," and she began to wipe her eyes.

"Poor old man! And me with a white-faced cow that I'm afraid of my life of, and an old horse that looks like a moth-eaten hide trunk we to have in our garret at home when I was a little girl, and belonged to my great-great-grandmother Atterson— —

"And there's a mess of chickens that eat all day long and don't lay an egg as far as I could see, besides a sow and a litter of six pigs that squeal worse than the the switch-engine down yonder in the freight yard— —

"And they're all to be fed, and how I'm to do it, and feed the boarders, too, I don't for the life of me see!" finished Mrs. Atterson, completely out of breath.

"What do you mean?" cried Hiram, suddenly waking to the significance of the old lady's chatter. "Do you mean he willed you these things?"

"Of course," she returned, smoothing down her best black skirt. "They go with the house and outbuildings—'all the chattels and appurtenances thereto', the will read."

"Why, Mrs. Atterson!" gasped Hiram. "He must have left you the farm."

"That's what I said," returned the old lady, complacently. "And what I'm to do with it I've no more idea than the man in the moon."

"A farm!" repeated Hiram, his face flushing and his eyes beginning to shine.

Now, Hiram Strong was not a particularly handsome youth, but in his excitement he almost looked so.

"Eighty acres, so many rods, and so many perches," pursued Mrs. Atterson, nodding. "That's the way it reads. The perches is in the henhouse, I s'pose—though why the description included them and not the hens' nests I dunno."

"Eighty acres of land!" repeated Hiram in a daze.

"All free and clear. Not a dollar against it—only encumbrances is the chickens, the cow, the horse and the pigs," declared Mrs. Atterson. "If it wasn't for them it might not be so bad. Scoville's an awfully nice place, and the farm's on an automobile road. A body needn't go blind looking for somebody to go by the door occasionally.

"And if it got so bad here finally that I couldn't make a livin' keeping boarders," pursued the lady, "I might go out there and live in the old house—which isn't much, I know, but it's a shelter, and my tastes are simple, goodness knows."

"But a farm, Mrs. Atterson!" broke in Hiram. "Think what you can do with it!"

"That's what I'd like to have, you, or somebody else tell me," exclaimed the old lady, tartly. "I ain't got no more use for a farm than a cat has for two tails!"

"But—but isn't it a good farm?" queried Hiram, puzzled.

"How do I know?" snapped the boarding house mistress. "I wouldn't know one farm from another, exceptin' two can't be in exactly the same spot. Oh! do you mean, could I sell it?"

"No——"

"The lawyer advised me not to sell just now. He said something about the state of the real estate market in that section. Prices would be better in a year or two. And then, the old place is mighty run down."

"That's what I mean," Hiram hastened to say. "Has it been cropped to death? Is the soil worn out? Can't you run it and make something out of it?"

"For pity's sake!" ejaculated the good lady, "how should I know? And I couldn't run it—I shouldn't know how.

"I've got a neighbor-woman in the house just now to 'tend to things—and that's costin' me a dollar and a half a week. And there'll be taxes to pay, and—and—Well, I just guess I'll have to try and sell it now and take what I can get.

"Though that lawyer says that if the place was fixed up a little and crops put in it would make a thousand dollars' difference in the selling price. That is, after a year or two.

"But bless us and save us" cried Mrs. Atterson, "I'd be swamped with expenses before that time."

"Mebbe not," said Hiram Strong, trying to repress his eagerness. "Why not try it?"

"Try to run that farm?" cried she. "Why, I'd jest as lief go up in one o' those aeroplanes and try to run it. I wouldn't be no more up in the air then than I would be on a farm," she added, grimly.

"Get somebody to run it for you—do the outside work, I mean, Mrs. Atterson," said Hiram. "You could keep house out there just as well as you do here. And it would be easy for you to learn to milk——" "That whitefaced cow? My goodness! I'd just as quick learn to milk a switch-engine!"

"But it's only her head that looks so wicked to you," laughed Hiram. "And you don't milk that end."

"Well—mebbe," admitted Mrs. Atterson, doubtfully. "I reckon I could make butter again—I used to do that when I was a girl at my aunt's. And either I'd make those hens lay or I'd have their dratted heads off!

"And my goodness me! To get rid of the boarders—Oh, stop your talkin', Hi Strong! That is too good to ever be true. Don't talk to me no more."

"But I want to talk to you, Mrs. Atterson," persisted the youth, eagerly.

"Well, who'd I get to do the outside work—put in crops, and 'tend 'em, and look out for that old horse?"

Hiram almost choked. This opportunity should not get past him if he could help it!

"Let me do it, Mrs. Atterson. Give me a chance to show you what I can do," he cried. "Let me run the farm for you!"

"Why—why do you suppose that it could be made to pay us, Hi?" demanded his landlady, in wonder.

"Other farms pay; why not this one?" rejoined Hiram, sententiously. "Of course," he added, his native caution coming to the surface, "I'd want to see the place—to look it over pretty well, in fact—before I made any agreement. And I can assure you, Mrs. Atterson, if I saw no chance of both you and me making something out of it I should tell you so."

"But—but your job, Hiram? And I wouldn't approve of your going out there and lookin' at the place on a Sunday."

"I'll take the early train Monday morning," said the youth, promptly.

"But what will they say at the store? Mr. Dwight— —"

"He turned me off to-day," said Hiram, steadily. "So I won't lose anything by going out there.

"I tell you what I'll do," he added briskly. "I won't have any too much money while I'm out of a job, of course. And I shall be out there at Scoville a couple of days looking the place over, it's probable.

"So, if you will let me keep this three dollars and a half I should pay you for my next week's board to-night, I'll pay my own expenses out there at the farm and if nothing comes of it, all well and good."

Mrs. Atterson had fumbled for her spectacles and now put them on to survey the boy's earnest face.

"Do you mean to say you can run a farm, Hi Strong?" she asked.

"I do," and he smiled confidently at her.

"And make it pay?"

"Perhaps not much profit the first season; but if the farm is fertile, and the marketing conditions are right, I know I can make it pay us both in two years."

"I've got a little money saved up. I could sell the house in a week, for it's always full and there are always lone women like me with a little driblet of money to exchange for a boarding house—heaven help us for the fools we are!" Mrs. Atterson exclaimed.

"And I expect you could raise vegetables enough to part keep us, Hi, even if the farm wasn't a great success?"

"And eggs, and chickens, and the pigs, and milk from the cow," suggested Hiram.

"Well! I declare, that's so," admitted Mrs. Atterson. "I'd been lookin' on all them things as an expense. They could be made an asset, eh?"

"I should hope so," responded Hiram, smiling.

"And I could get rid of these boarders—My soul and body!" gasped the tired woman, suddenly. "Do you suppose it's true, Hi? Get rid of worryin' about paying the bills, and whether the boarders are all going to keep their jobs and be able to pay regularly—And the gravy!

"Hiram Strong! If you can show me a way out of this valley of tribulation I'll be the thankfullest woman that you ever seen. It's a bargain. Don't you pay me a cent for this coming week. And I shouldn't have taken it, anyway, when you're throwed out of work so. That's a mighty mean man, that Daniel Dwight.

"You go right ahead and look that farm over. If it looks good, you come back and we'll strike a bargain, I know. And—and—Just to think of getting rid of this house and these boarders!" and Mrs. Atterson finished by wiping her eyes again vigorously.

CHAPTER VII
HOW HIRAM LEFT TOWN

Hiram Strong was up betimes on Monday morning—Sister saw to that. She rapped on his door at four-thirty.

Sometimes Hiram wondered when the girl ever slept. She was still dragging about the kitchen or dining-room when he went to bed, and she was first down in the morning—even earlier than Mrs. Atterson herself.

The boarding house mistress was not intentionally severe with Sister; but the much harassed lady had never learned to make her own work easy, so how should she be expected to be easy on Sister?

Once or twice Hiram had talked with the orphan. Sister had a dreadful fear of returning to the "institution" from which Mrs. Atterson had taken her. And Sister's other fearful remembrance was of an old woman who beat her and drank much gin and water.

Not that she had been ill-treated at the institution; but she had been dressed in an ugly uniform, and the girls had been rough and pulled her "pigtails" like Dan, Junior.

"Once a gentleman came to see me," Sister confided to Hiram. "He was a lawyer gentleman, the matron told me. He knew my name—but I've forgotten it now.

"And he said that somebody who once belonged to me—or I once belonged to them—had died and perhaps there would be some money coming to me. But it couldn't have been the old woman I lived with, for she never had only money enough for gin!

"Anyhow, I was glad. I axed him how much money—was it enough to treat all the girls in the institution one round of ice-cream soda, and he laffed, he did. And he said yes—just about enough for that, if he could get it for me. And I ran away and told the girls.

"I promised them all a treat. But the man never came again, and by and by the big girls said they believed I storied about it, and one night they came and dragged me out of bed and hung me out of the window by my wrists, till I thought my arms would be pulled right out of the sockets. They was awful cruel—them girls. But when I axed the matron why the man didn't come no more, she put me off. I guess he was only foolin'," decided Sister, with a sigh. "Folks like to fool me—like Mr. Crackit—eh?"

But Mrs. Atterson told Hiram, when he asked about Sister's meagre little story, that the institution had promised to let her know if the lawyer ever returned to make further inquiries about the orphan. Somebody really had died who was of kin to the girl, but through some error the institution had not made a proper record of her pedigree and the lawyer who had instituted the search a seemed to have dropped out of sight.

But Hiram was not troubled by poor Sister's private affairs upon this Monday morning. It was the beginning of a new week, indeed, to him. He had turned over a new leaf of experience. He hoped that he was pretty near to the end of his harsh city existence.

He hurried downstairs, long in advance of the other boarders, and Mrs. Atterson served him some breakfast, although there was no milk for the coffee.

"I dunno where that plague o' my life, Sister's, gone," sputtered the old lady, fussing about, between dining-room and kitchen. "I sent her out ten minutes ago for the milk. And if you want to get that first train to Scoville you've got to hurry."

"Never mind the milk," laughed the young fellow. "The train's more important this morning."

So he bolted the remainder of his breakfast, swallowed the black coffee, and ran out.

He arrived at Scoville while the morning was still young. It was not his intention to go at once to the Atterson farm. There were matters which he desired to look into in addition to judging the quality of the soil on the place and the possibility of making it pay.

He went to the storekeepers and asked questions about the prices paid for garden truck. He walked about the town and saw the quality of the residences, and noted what proportion of the townsfolk cultivated gardens of their own.

There was a big girls' boarding-school, and two small, but well-patronized hotels. The proprietors of these each owned a farm; but they told Hiram that it was necessary for them to buy much of their table vegetables from city produce men, as the neighboring farmers did not grow much.

In talking with one storekeeper Hiram mentioned the fact that he was going to look at the Atterson place with a view to farming it for its new owner. When he walked out of the store he found himself accosted by a lean, snaky-looking man who had stood within the store the moment before.

"What's this widder woman goin' to do with the farm old Jeptha left her?" inquired the man, looking at Hiram slyly.

"We don't know yet, sir, what we shall do with it," the young fellow replied.

"You her son?"

"No. I may work for her—can't tell till I've looked at the place."

"It ain't much to look at," said the man, quickly. "I come near buying it once, though. In fact—"

He hesitated, still eyeing Hiram sideways. The boy waited for him to speak again. He did not wish to be impolite; but he did not like the man's appearance.

"What do y' reckon this Mis' Atterson would sell for?" finally demanded the man.

"She has been advised not to sell—at present."

"Who by?"

"Mr. Strickland, the lawyer."

"Humph! Mebbe I'd buy it—and give her a good price for it—right now."

"What do you consider a good price?" asked Hiram, quietly.

"Twelve hundred dollars," said the man.

"I will tell her. But I do not think she would sell for that price—nothing like it, in fact."

"Well, mebbe she'll feel different when she comes to think it over. No use for a woman trying to run a farm. And if she has to pay for everything to be done, she'll be in a hole at the end of the season. I guess she ain't thought of that?"

"It wouldn't be my place to point it out to her," returned Hiram, "coolly, if it were so, and I wanted to work for her."

"Humph! Mebbe not. Well, my name's Pepper. Mebbe I'll be out to see her some day," he said, and turned away.

"He's one of the people who will discourage Mrs. Atterson," thought Hiram. "And he has an axe to grind. If I decide to take the job of making this farm pay, I'm going to have the agreement in black and white with Mrs. Atterson; for there will be a raft of Job's comforters, perhaps when we get settled on the place."

It was late in the afternoon before Hiram was ready to start for the farm itself. He had made some enquiries, and had decided to stop at a neighbor's for overnight, instead of going to the house where a lone woman had been left in charge by Mrs. Atterson.

The Pollocks had been recommended to Hiram, and by leaving the road within half a mile of the Atterson farm, and cutting across the fields, he came into the dooryard of the Pollock place. A well-grown boy, not much older than himself, was splitting some chunks at the woodpile. He stopped work to gaze at the visitor with much curiosity.

"From what they told me in town," Hi said, holding out his hand with a smile, "you must be Henry Pollock?"

The boy blushed, but awkwardly took and shook Hi's hand.

"That's what they call me—Henry Pollock—when they don't call me Hen."

"Well, I'll make a bargain with you, Henry," laughed Hiram. "I don't like to have my name cut off short, either. My name's Hiram Strong. So if you'll agree to always call me `Hiram' I'll always call you `Henry.'"

"It's a go!" returned the other, shaking hands again. "You going to live around here? Or are you jest visiting?"

"I don't know yet," confessed Hiram, sitting down beside the boy. "You see, I've come out to look at the Atterson place."

"That's right over yonder. You can see the roof if you stand up," said Henry, quickly.

Hiram stood up and, in the light of the early sunset, he caught a glimpse of the roof in question.

"Your folks going to buy it of the old lady Uncle Jeptha left it to?" asked Henry, with pardonable curiosity. "Or are you going to rent it?"

"What do you think of renting it?" queried Hiram, showing that he had Yankee blood in him by answering one question with another.

"Well—it's pretty well run down, and that's a fact. The old man couldn't do much the last few years, and them Dickersons who farmed it for him ain't no great shakes of farmers, now I tell you!"

"Well, I want to look the farm over before I decide what I'll do," said Hiram, slowly. "And of course I can't do that to-night. They told me in town that sometimes you take boarders?"

"In the summer we do," returned Henry.

"Do you think your folks will put me up overnight?"

"Why, I reckon so—Hiram Strong, did you say your name was? Come right in," added Henry, hospitably, "and I'll ask mother."

CHAPTER VIII
THE LURE OF GREEN FIELDS

The Pollocks proved to be a neighborly family—and a large one. As Henry said, there was a "whole raft of young 'uns" younger than he was. They made Hiram very welcome at the supper table, and showed much curiosity about his personal affairs.

But the young fellow had been used to just such people before. They were not a bad sort, and if they were keenly interested in the affairs of other people, it was because they had few books and newspapers, and small chance to amuse themselves in the many ways which city people have.

Hiram slept with Henry that night, and Henry agreed to show the visitor over the Atterson place the next day.

"I know every stick and stone of it as well as I do ourn," declared Henry. "And Dad won't mind my taking time now. Later—Whew! I tell you, we hafter just git up an' dust to make a crop. Not much chance for fun after a week or two until the corn's laid by."

"You know all the boundaries of the Atterson farm, do you?" Hiram asked.

"Yes, sir!" replied Henry, eagerly. "And say! do you like to fish?"

"Of course; who doesn't?"

"Then we'll take some lines and hooks along—and mother'll lend us a pan and kettle. Say! We'll start early—'fore anybody's a-stir—and I bet there'll be a big trout jumping in the pool under the big sycamore."

"That certain-sure sounds good to me!" cried Hiram, enthusiastically.

So it was agreed, and before day, while the mist was yet rolling across the fields, and the hedge sparrows were beginning to chirp, the two set forth from the Pollock place, crossed the wet fields, and the road, and set off down the slope of a long hill, following, as Henry said, near the east boundary of the Atterson farm—the line running from the automobile road to the river.

It was a dull spring morning. The faint breeze that stirred on the hillside was damp, but odorous with new-springing herbs. As Hiram and Henry descended the aisle of the pinewood, the treetops whispered together as though curious of these bold humans who disturbed their solitude.

"It doesn't look as though anybody had been here at the back end of old Jeptha Atterson's farm for years," said Hiram.

"And it's a fact that nobody gets down this way often," Henry responded.

The brown tags sprung under their feet; now and then a dew-wet branch swept Hiram's cheek, seeking with its cold fingers to stay his progress. It was an enchanted forest, and the boy, heart-hungry from his two years of city life, was enchanted, too!

Hiram learned from talking with his companion that at one time the piece of thirty-year-old timber they were walking through had been tilled — after a fashion. But it had never been properly cleared, as the hacked and ancient stumpage betrayed.

Here and there the lines of corn rows which had been plowed when the last crop was laid by were plainly revealed to Hiram's observing eye. Where corn had grown once, it should grow again; and the pine timber would more than pay for being cut, for blowing out the big stumps with dynamite, and tam-harrowing the side hill.

Finally they reached a point where the ground fell away more abruptly and the character of the timber changed, as well. Instead of the stately pines, this more abrupt declivity was covered with hickory and oak. The sparse brush sprang out of rank, black mold.

Charmed by the prospect, Hiram and Henry descended this hill and came suddenly, through a fringe of brush, to the border of an open cove, or bottom.

At some time this lowland, too, had been cleared and cultivated; but now young pines, quick-springing and lush, dotted the five or six acres of practically open land which was as level as one's palm.

It was two hundred yards, or more, in width and at the farther side a hedge of alders and pussywillows grew, with the green mist of young leaves upon them, and here and there a ghostly sycamore, stretching its slender bole into the air, edged the course of the river.

Hiram viewed the scene with growing delight. His eyes sparkled and a smile came to his lips as he crossed, with springy steps, the open meadow on which the grass was already showing green in patches.

Between the line of the wood they had left and the breadth of the meadow was a narrow, marshy strip into which a few stones had been cast, and on these they crossed dry shod. The remainder of the bottom-land was firm.

"Ain't this jest a scrumptious place?" demanded Henry, and Hiram agreed.

At the river's edge they parted the bushes and looked down upon the oily-flowing brown flood. It was some thirty feet broad and with the melting of the snows in the mountains was so deep that no sign was apparent here of the rocks which covered its bed.

Henry led the way up the bank of the stream toward a huge sycamore that leaned lovingly over the water. An ancient wild grape vine, its butt four inches through and its roots fairly in the water, had a strangle-hold upon this decrepit forest monarch, its tendrils reaching the sycamore's topmost branch.

Under the tree was a deep hole where flotsam leaves and twigs performed an endless treadmill dance in the grasp of the eddy.

Suddenly, while their gaze clung to the dimpling water, there was a flash of a bronze body—a streak of light along the surface of the pool—and two widening circles showed where the master of the hole had leaped for some insect prey.

"See him?" called Henry, but under his breath.

Hiram nodded, but squeezed his companion's hand for silence. He almost held his own breath for the moment, as they moved back from the pool with the soundless step of an Indian.

"That big feller is my meat," declared Henry.

"Go to it, boy!" urged Hiram, and set about preparing the camp.

He cut with his big jack-knife and set up a tripod of green rods in a jiffy, skirmished for dry wood, lit his fire, filled the kettle from the river at a little distance from the eddy, and hung it over the blaze to boil.

Meanwhile Henry fished out a line and an envelope of hooks from an inner pocket, cut a springy pole back on the hillside, rigged his line and hook, and kicked a hole in the soft, rich soil until he unearthed a fat angleworm.

With this impaled upon the hook he cautiously approached the pool under the sycamore and cast gently. The struggling worm sank slowly; the water wrinkled about the line; but there followed no tug at the hook, although Henry stood patiently for several moments. He cast again, and yet again, with like result.

"Ah, ba!" muttered Hiram, in his ear; "this fellow's appetite needs tickling. He is being fed too well and turns up his nose at a common earthworm, does he? Let me show you a wrinkle, Henry."

Henry drew the line ashore again and shook off the useless bait.

"You're, not fishing," Hiram continued with a grim smile. "You've just been drowning a worm. But I'll show that old fellow sulking down below there that he is no match this early in the spring for a pair of hungry boys!"

He recrossed the meadow, and the stepping stones, to the wood. He had noticed a log lying in the path as he descended the hillside. With the toe of his boot he kicked a patch of bark from the log, and thereby lay bare the wavering trail of a busy grub. Following the trail he quickly found the fat, juicy insect, which immediately took the earthworm's place upon the hook.

Again Henry cast and this time, before the grub even touched the surface of the pool, the fish leaped and swallowed the tempting morsel, hook and all!

There was no playing of the fish on Henry's part. A quick jerk and the gasping spotted beauty, a pound and a quarter, or more, in weight, lay upon the sward beside the crackling fire.

"Whoop-ee!" called Henry, excitedly. "That's Number One!"

While Hiram dexterously scaled and cleaned the first trout, Henry caught a couple more. Hiram brought forth, too, the coffee, salt and pepper, sugar, a piece of fat salt pork and two table knives and forks.

He raked a smooth bed in the glowing coals, sliced the pork thin, laid some slices in the pan and set that upon the coals, where the pork began to sputter almost at once.

The water in the kettle was boiling and he made the coffee. Then he laid the trout upon the pan with three slices of pork upon each, and sat back upon his haunches beside Henry enjoying the delicious odor in anticipation of the more solid delights of breakfast.

They had hard crackers and with these, and drinking the coffee from the kettle itself, when it was cool enough, the two boys feasted like monarchs.

"By Jo!" exclaimed Henry. "This beats maw's soda biscuit and fat meat gravy!"

But as he ate, Hiram's gaze traveled again and again across the scrub-grown meadow. The lay of the land pleased him. The richness of the soil had been revealed when they dug the earthworm.

For thousands of years the riches of yonder hillside had been washing down upon the bottom, and this alluvial was rich beyond computation.

Here were several acres, the young farmer knew, which, however over-cropped the remainder of Uncle Jeptha's land had been, could not be impoverished in many seasons.

"It's as rich as cream!" muttered he, thoughtfully. "Grubbing out these young pines wouldn't take long. There's a heavy sod and it would have to be ploughed deeply. Then a crop of corn this year, perhaps—late corn for fear the river might overflow it in June. And then— —

"Great Scot!" ejaculated Hiram, slapping his knee, "what wouldn't grow on this bottom land?"

"Yes, it's mighty rich," agreed Henry. "But it's a long way from the house—and then, the river might flood it over. I've seen water running over this bottom two feet deep—once."

They finished the al fresco meal and Hiram leaped up, inspired by his thoughts to brisker movements.

"Whatever else this old farm has on it, I vow and declare," he said, "this five or six acres alone might be made to pay a profit on the whole investment!"

CHAPTER IX
THE BARGAIN IS MADE

Henry showed Hiram the "branch", a little stream flowing into the river, which marked the westerly boundary of the farm for some ways, and they set off up the steep bank of this stream.

This back end of the farm—quite forty acres, or half of the whole tract—had been entirely neglected by the last owner of the property for a great many years. It was some distance from the house, for the farm was a long and narrow strip of land from the highway to the river, and Uncle Jeptha had had quite all he could do to till the uplands and the fields adjacent to his home.

They came upon these open fields—many of them filthy with dead weeds and littered with sprouting bushes—from the rear. Hiram saw that the fences were in bad repair and that the back of the premises gave every indication of neglect and shiftlessness.

Perhaps not exactly the latter; Uncle Jeptha had been an old man and unable to do much active work for some years. But he had cropped certain of his fields "on shares" with the usual results—impoverished soil, illy-tilled crops, and the land left in a slovenly condition which several years of careful tillage would hardly overcome.

Now, although Hiram's father had been of the tenant class, he had farmed other men's land as he would his own. Owners of outlying farms had been glad to get Mr. Strong to till their fields.

He had known how to work, he knew the reasons for every bit of labor he performed, and he had not kept his son in ignorance of them. As they worked together the father had explained to the son what he did, and why he did it, The results of their work spoke for themselves, and Hiram had a retentive memory.

Mr. Strong, too, had been a great, reader—especially in the winter when the farmer naturally has more time in-doors.

Yet he was a "twelve months farmer"; he knew that the winter, despite the broken nature of the work, was quite as valuable to the successful farmer as the other seasons of the year.

The elder Strong knew that men with more money, and more time for experimenting than he had, were writing and publishing all the time helps for the wise farmer. He subscribed for several papers, and read and digested them carefully.

Hiram, even during his two years in the city, had continued his subscription (although it was hard to find the money sometimes) to two or three of those publications that his father had most approved. And the boy had read them faithfully.

He was as up-to-date in farming lore now, if not in actual practise, as he had been when he left the country to try his fortune in Crawberry.

Beyond the place where the branch turned back upon itself and hid its source in the thicker timber, Hiram saw that the fields were open on both sides of this westerly line of the farm.

"Who's our neighbor over yonder, Henry?" he asked.

"Dickerson—Sam Dickerson," said Henry. "And he's got a boy, Pete, no older than us. Say, Hiram, you'll have trouble with Pete Dickerson."

"Oh, I guess not," returned the young farmer, laughing. "Trouble is something that I don't go about hunting for."

"You don't have to hunt it when Pete is round," said Henry with a wry grin. "But mebbe he won't bother you, for he's workin' near town—for that new man that's moved into the old Fleigler place. Bronson's his name. But if Pete don't bother you, Sam may."

"Sam's the father?"

"Yep. And one poor farmer and mean man, if ever there was one! Oh, Pete comes by his orneriness honestly enough."

"Oh, I hope I'll have no trouble with any neighbor," said Hiram, hopefully.

They came briskly to the outbuildings belonging to Mrs. Atterson's newly acquired legacy. Hiram glanced into the hog lot. She looked like a good sow, and the six-weeks-old shoats were in good condition. In a couple of weeks they would be big enough to sell if Mrs. Atterson did not care to raise them.

The shoats were worth six dollars a pair, too; he had inquired the day before about them. There was practically eighteen dollars squealing in that pen—and eighteen dollars would go a long way toward feeding the horse and cow until there was good pasturage for them.

These animals named were in the small fenced barnyard. In the fall and winter the old man had fed a good deal of fodder and other roughage, and during the winter the horse and cow had tramped this coarse material, and the stable scrapings, into a mat of fairly good manure.

He looked the horse and cow over with more care. It was a fact that the horse looked pretty shaggy; but he had been used little during the winter, and had been seldom curried. A ragged coat upon a horse sometimes covers quite as many good points as the same quality of garment does upon a man.

When Hiram spoke to the beast it came to the fence with a friendly forward thrust of its ears, and the confidence of a horse that has been kindly treated and looks upon even a strange human as a friend.

It was a strong and well-shaped animal, more than twelve years old, as Hiram discovered when he opened the creature's mouth, but seemingly sound in limb. Nor was he too large for work on the cultivator, while sturdy enough to carry a single plow.

Hiram passed him over with a satisfactory pat on the nose and turned to look at the white-faced cow that had so terrified Mrs. Atterson. She wasn't a bad looking beast, either, and would freshen shortly. Her calf would be worth from twelve to fifteen dollars if Mrs. Atterson did not wish to raise it. Another future asset to mention to the old lady when he returned.

The youth turned his attention to the buildings themselves—the barn, the cart shed, the henhouse, and the smaller buildings. That famous old decorating firm of Wind & Weather had contracted for all painting done around the Atterson place for the many years; but the buildings were not otherwise in a bad state of repair.

A few shingles had been blown off the roofs; here and there a board was loose. With a hammer and a few nails, and in a few hours, many of these small repairs could be accomplished. And a coat or two of properly mixed and applied whitewash would freshen up the whole place and—like charity—cover a multitude of sins.

Henry bade him good-bye now, they shook hands, and Hiram agreed to let his new friend know at once if he decided to come with Mrs. Atterson to the farm.

"We can have heaps of fun—you and me," declared Henry.

"It isn't so bad," soliloquized the young farmer when he was alone. "There'd be time to put the buildings and fences in good shape before the spring work came on with a rush. There's fertilizer enough in the barnyard and the pig pen and the hen run—with the help of a few pounds of salts and some bone meal, perhaps—to enrich a right smart kitchen garden and spread for corn on that four acre lot yonder.

"Of course, this land up here on the hill needs humus. If it has been cropped on shares, as Henry says, all the enrichment it has received has been from commercial fertilizers. And necessarily they have made the land sour. It probably needs lime badly.

"Yes, I can't encourage Mrs. Atterson to look for a profit in anything this year. It will take a year to get that rich bottom into shape for—for what, I wonder? Onions? Celery? It would raise 'em both. I'll think about that and look over the market prospects more fully before I decide."

For already, you see, Hiram had come to the decision that this old farm could be made to pay. Why not? The true farmer has to have imagination as well as the knowledge and the perseverance to grow crops. He must be able in his mind's eye to see a field ready for the reaping before he puts in a seed.

He did not go to the house on this occasion, but after casually examining the tools and harness, and the like, left by the old man, he cut off across the upper end of the farm and gave the neglected open fields of this upper forty a casual examination.

"If she had the money to invest, I'd say buy sheep and fence these fields and so get rid of the weeds. They've grown very foul through neglect, and cultivating them for years would not destroy the weeds as sheep would in two seasons.

"But wire fencing is expensive—and so are good sheep to begin with. No. Slow but sure must be our motto. I mustn't advise any great outlay of money—that would scare her to death.

"It will be hard enough for her to put out money all season long before there are any returns. We'll go, slow," repeated Hiram.

But when he left the farm that afternoon he went swiftly enough to Scoville and took the train for the not far distant city of Crawberry. This was Tuesday evening and he arrived just about supper time at Mrs. Atterson's.

The reason for Hiram's absence, and the matter of Mrs. Atterson's legacy altogether, had been kept from the boarders. And there was no time until after the principal meal of the day was off the lady's mind for Hiram to say anything to her.

"She's a good old soul," thought Hiram. "And if it's in my power to make that farm pay, and yield her a competency for her old age, I'll do it."

Meanwhile he was not losing sight of the fact that there was something due to him in this matter. He was bound to see that he got his share—and a just share—of any profits that might accrue from the venture.

So, after the other boarders had scattered, and Mrs. Atterson had eaten her own late supper, and Sister was swashing plates and knives and forks about in a big pan of hot water in the kitchen sink, (between whiles doing her best to listen at the crack of the door) the landlady and Hiram Strong threshed out the project fully.

It was not all one-sided; for Mrs. Atterson, after all, had been bargaining all her life and could see the "main chance" as quickly as the next one. She had not bickered with hucksters, chivvied grocerymen, fought battles royal with butchers, and endured the existence of a Red Indian amidst allied foes for two decades without having her wits ground to a razor edge.

On the other hand, Hiram Strong, although a boy in years, had been his own master long enough to take care of himself in most transactions, and withal had a fund of native caution. They jotted down memoranda of the points on which they were agreed, which included the following:

Mrs. Atterson, as "party of the first part", agreed to board Hiram until the crops were harvested the second year. In addition she was to pay him one hundred dollars at Christmas time this first year, and another hundred at the conclusion of the agreement—i. e., when the second year's crop was harvested.

Beside, of the estimated profits of the second year's crop, Hiram was to have twenty-five per cent. This profit was to be that balance in the farm's favor (if such balance there was) over and above the actual cost of labor, seed, and such purchased fertilizer or other supplies as were necessary. Mrs. Atterson agreed likewise to supply one serviceable horse and such tools as might be needed, for the place was to be run as "a one-horse farm."

On the other hand Hiram agreed to give his entire time to the farm, to work for Mrs. Atterson's interest in all things, to make no expenditures without discussing them first with her, and to give his best care and attention generally to the farm and all that pertained thereto. Of course, the old lady was taking Hiram a good deal on trust. But she had known the boy almost two years and he had been faithful and prompt in discharging his debts to her.

But it was up to the young fellow to "make good." He could not expect to make any profit for his employer the first year; but he would be expected to do so the second season, or "show cause."

When these matters were all discussed and the little memorandum signed, Hiram Strong, in his own room, thought the situation over very seriously. He was facing the biggest responsibility that he had obliged to assume in his whole life.

This was no boyish job; it was man's work. He had put his hand to an agreement that might influence his whole future, and certainly would make or break his credit as a trustworthy youth and one of his word.

During these past days Hiram had determined to "get back to the soil" and to get back to it in a business-like way. He desired to make good for Mrs. Atterson so that he might some time have the chance to make good for somebody else on a bigger scale.

He did not propose to be "a one-horse farmer" all his days.

CHAPTER X
THE SOUND OF BEATING HOOFS

On Monday morning Mrs. Atterson put her house in the agent's hands. On Wednesday a pair of spinster ladies came to look at it. They came again on Thursday and again on Friday.

Friday being considered an "unlucky" day they did not bind the bargain; but on Saturday money was passed, and the new keepers of the house were to take possession in a week. Not until then were the boarders informed of Mother Atterson's change of circumstances, and the fact that she was going to graduate from the boarding house kitchen to the farm.

After all, they were sorry—those light-headed, irresponsible young men. There wasn't one of them, from Crackit down the line, who could not easily remember some special kindness that marked the old lady's intercourse with him.

As soon as the fact was announced that the boarding house had changed hands, the boarders were up in arms. There was a wild gabble of voices, over the supper table that night. Crackit led the chorus.

"It's a mean trick. Mother Atterson has sold us like so many cattle to the highest bidder. Ungrateful—right down ungrateful, I call it," he declared. "What do you say, Feeble?"

"It is particularly distasteful to me just now," complained the invalid. "When Sister has learned to give me my hot water at just the right temperature," and he took a sip of that innocent beverage. "Don't you suppose we could prevail upon the old lady to renig?"

"She's bound to put us off with half rations for the rest of the time she stays," declared Crackit, shaking his head wisely. "She's got nothing to lose now. She don't care if we all up and leave—after she gets hers."

"That's always the way," feebly remarked Mr. Peebles. "Just as soon as I really get settled down into a half-decent lodging, something happens."

Mr. Peebles had been a fixture at Mother Atterson's for nearly ten years. Only Old Lem Camp had been longer at the place.

The latter was the only boarder who had no adverse criticism for the mistress's new move. Indeed this evening Mr. Camp said nothing whatever; even his usual mumblings to himself were not heard.

He ate slowly, and but little. He was still sitting at the table when all the others had departed.

Mrs. Atterson started into the dining-room with her own supper between two plates when she saw the old man sitting there despondent in looks and attitude, his head resting on one clawlike hand, his elbow on the soiled table cloth.

He did not look up, nor move. The mistress glanced back over her shoulder, and there was Sister, sniffling and occasionally rubbing her wrist into her red eyes as she scraped the tower of plates from the dinner table.

"My soul and body!" gasped Mother Atterson, almost dropping her supper on the floor. "There's Sister—and there's Old Lem Camp! Whatever will I do with 'em?"

Meanwhile Hiram Strong had already left for the farm on the Wednesday previous. The other boarders knew nothing about his agreement with Mother Atterson; he had agreed to go to the place and begin work, and take care of the stock and all, "choring for himself", as the good lady called it, until she could complete her city affairs and move herself and her personal chattels to the farm.

Hiram bore a note to the woman who had promised to care for the Atterson place, and money to pay her what the boarding-house mistress had agreed.

"You can 'bach' it in the house as well as poor old Uncle Jeptha did, I reckon," this woman told the youth.

She showed him where certain provisions were—the pork barrel, ham and bacon of the old man's curing, and the few vegetables remaining from the winter's store.

"The cow was about gone dry, anyway," said the woman, Mrs. Larriper, who was a widow and lived with her married daughter some half-mile down the road toward Scoville, "so I didn't bother to milk her.

"You'll have to go to town to buy grain, if you want to feed her up—and for the chickens and the horse. The old man didn't make much of a crop last year—or them shiftless Dickersons didn't make much for him.

"I saw Sam Dickerson around here this morning. He borrowed some of the old man's tools when Uncle Jeptha was sick, and you'll have to go after 'em, I reckon.

"Sam's the best borrower that ever was; but he never can remember to bring things back. He says it's bad enough to have to borrow; it's too much to expect the same man to return what he borrows.

"Now, Mrs. Dickerson," pursued Mrs. Larriper, "was as nice a girl before she married—she was a Stepney—as ever walked in shoe-leather. And I guess she'd be right friendly with the neighbors if Sam would let her.

"But the poor thing never gits to go out—no, sir! She's jest tied to the house. They lost a child once—four year ago. That's the only time I remember of seeing Sarah Stepney in church since the day she was married—and she's got a boy—Pete—as old as you be.

"Now, on the other side o' ye there's Darrell's tract, and you won't have no trouble there, for there ain't a house on his place, and he lets it lie idle. Waiting for a rise in price, I 'spect.

"Some rich folks is comin' in and buying up pieces of land and making what they calls 'gentlemen's estates' out o' them. A family named Bronson— Mr. Stephen Bronson, with one little girl—bought the Fleigler place only last month.

"They're nice folks," pursued this amiable but talkative lady, "and they don't live but a mile or so along the Scoville road. You passed the place— white, with green shutters, and a water-tower in the back, when you walked up."

"I remember it," said Hiram, nodding.

"They're western folk. Come clear from out in Injiany, or Illiny, or the like. The girl's going to school and she ain't got no mother, so her father's come on East with her to be near the school.

"Well, I can't help you no more. Them hens! Well, I'd sell 'em if I was Mis' Atterson.

"Hens ain't much nowadays, anyhow; and I expect a good many of those are too old to lay. Uncle Jeptha couldn't fuss with chickens, and he didn't raise only a smitch of 'em last year and the year before—just them that the hens hatched themselves in stolen nests, and chanced to bring up alive.

"You better grease the cart before you use it. It's stood since they hauled in corn last fall.

"And look out for Dickerson. Ask him for the things he borrowed. You'll need 'em, p'r'aps, if you're goin' to do any farmin' for Mis' Atterson."

She bustled away. Hiram thought he had heard enough about his neighbors for a while, and he went out to look over the pasture fencing, which was to be his first repair job. He would have that ready to turn the cow and her calf into as soon as the grass began to grow.

He rummaged about in what had been half woodshed and half workshop in Uncle Jeptha's time, and found a heavy claw-hammer, a pair of wire cutters, and a pocket full of fence staples.

With this outfit he prepared to follow the line fence, which was likewise the pasture fence on the west side, between Mrs. Atterson's and Dickerson's.

Where he could, he mended the broken strands of wire. In other places the wires had sagged and were loose. The claw-hammer fixed these like a charm. Slipping the wire into the claw, a single twist of the wrist would usually pick up the sag and make the wire taut again at that point.

He drove a few staples, as needed, as he walked along. The pasture partook of the general conformation of the farm—it was rather long and narrow.

It had grown to clumps of bushes in spots, and there was sufficient shade. But he did not come to the water until he reached the lower end of the lot.

The branch trickled from a spring, or springs, farther east. It made an elbow at the corner of the pasture—the lower south-west corner—and there a water-hole had been scooped out at some past time.

This waterhole was deep enough for all purposes, and was shaded by a great oak that had stood there long before the house belonging to Jeptha Atterson had been built.

Here Hiram struck something that puzzled him. The boundary fence crossed this water-hole at a tangent, and recrossed to the west bank of the outflowing branch a few yards below, leaving perhaps half of the water-hole upon the neighbor's side of the fence.

Some of this wire at the water-hole was practically new. So were the posts. And after a little Hiram traced the line of old postholes which had followed a straight line on the west side of the water-hole.

In other words, this water-privilege for Dickerson's land was of recent arrangement—so recent indeed, that the young farmer believed he could see some fresh-turned earth about the newly-set posts.

"That's something to be looked into, I am afraid," thought Hiram, as he moved along the southern pasture fence.

But the trickle of the branch beckoned him; he had not found the fountain-head of the little stream when he had walked over a part of the timbered land with Henry Pollock, and now he struck into the open woods again, digging into the soil here and there with his heavy boot, marking the quality and age of the timber, and casting-up in his mind the possibilities and expense of clearing these overgrown acres.

"Mrs. Atterson may have a very valuable piece of land here in time," muttered Hiram. "A sawmill set up in here could cut many a hundred thousand feet of lumber—and good lumber, too. But it would spoil the beauty of the farm."

However, as must ever be in the case of the utility farm, the house was set on its ugliest part. The cleared fields along the road had nothing but the background of woods on the south and east to relieve their monotony.

On the brow of the steeper descent, which he had noted on his former visit to the back end of the farm, he found a certain clearing in the wood. Here the pines surrounded the opening on three sides.

To the south, through a break in the wooded hillside, he obtained a far-reaching view of the river valley as it lay, to the east and to the west. The prospect was delightful.

Here and there, on the farther bank of the river, which rose less abruptly there than on this side, lay several cheerful looking farmsteads. The white dwellings and outbuildings dotted the checkered fields of green and brown.

Cowbells tinkled in the distance, for the weather tempted farmers to let their cattle run in the pastures even so early in the season. A horse whinnied shrilly to a mate in a distant field.

The creaking of the heavy wheels of a laden farm-cart was a mellow sound in Hiram's ears. Beyond a fir plantation, high on the hillside, the sharply outlined steeple of a little church lay against the soft blue horizon.

"A beauty-spot!" Hiram muttered. "What a site for a home! And yet people want to build their houses right on an automobile road, and in sight of the rural mail box!"

His imagination began to riot, spurred by the outlook and by the nearer prospect of wood and hillside. The sun now lay warmly upon him as he sat upon a stump and drank in the beauty of it all.

After a time his ear, becoming attuned to the multitudinous voices of the wood, descried the silvery note of falling water. He arose and traced the sound.

Less than twenty yards away, and not far from the bluff, a vigorous rivulet started from beneath the half-bared roots of a monster beech, and fell over an outcropping boulder into a pool so clear that sand on its bottom, worked mysteriously into a pattern by the action of the water, lay revealed.

Hiram knelt on a mossy rock beside the pool, and bending put his lips to the water. It was the sweetest, most satisfying drink, he had imbibed for many a day.

But the morning was growing old, and Hiram wanted to trace the farther line of the farm. He went down to the river, crossed the open meadow again where they had built the campfire the morning before, and found the deeply scarred oak which stood exactly on the boundary line between the Atterson and Darrell tracts.

He turned to the north, and followed the line as nearly as might be. The Darrell tract was entirely wooded, and when he reached the uplands he kept on in the shadowy aisles of the sap-pines which covered his neighbor's property.

He came finally to where the ground fell away again, and the yellow, deeply-rutted road lay at his feet. The winter had played havoc with the automobile track.

The highway was unfenced and the bank dropped fifteen feet to the beaten path. A leaning oak overhung the road and Hiram lingered here, lying on its broad trunk, face upward, with his hat pulled over his eyes to shield them from the sunlight which filtered through the branches.

This land hereabout was beautiful. The boy could appreciate the beauty as well as the utility of the soil. It was so pleasing to the eye that he wished with all his heart it had been his own land he had surveyed.

"And I'll not be a tenant farmer all my life, nor a farm-foreman, as father was," determined the boy. "I'll get ahead. If I work for the benefit of other people for a few years, surely I'll win the chance in time to at last work for myself."

In the midst of his ruminations a sound broke upon his ear—a jarring note in the peaceful murmur of the woodland life. It was the thud of a horse's hoofs.

Not the sedate tunk-tunk of iron-shod feet on the damp earth, but an erratic and rapid pounding of hoof-beats which came on with such startling swiftness that Hiram sat up instantly, and craned his neck to see up the road.

"That horse is running away!" gasped the young farmer, and he swung himself out upon the lowest branch of the leaning tree which overhung the carttrack, the better to see along the highway.

CHAPTER XI
A GIRL RIDES INTO THE TALE

There was no bend in the highway for some distance, but the overhanging trees masked the track completely, save for a few hundred yards. The horse, whether driven or running at large, was plainly spurred by fright.

Into the peacefulness of this place its hoof-beats were bringing the element of peril.

Lying prostrate on the sloping trunk, Hiram could see much farther up the road. The outstretched head and lathered breast of a tall bay horse leaped into view, and like a picture in a kinetoscope, growing larger and more vivid second by second, the maddened animal came down the road.

Hiram could see that the beast was not riderless, but it was a moment or two—a long-drawn, anxious space of heart-beaten seconds—ere he realized what manner of rider it was who clung so desperately to the masterless creature.

"It's a girl—a little girl!" gasped Hiram.

She was only a speck of color, with white, drawn face, on the back of the racing horse.

Every plunge of the oncoming animal shook the little figure as though it must fall from the saddle. But Hiram could see that she hung with phenomenal pluck to the broken bridle and to the single horn of her side-saddle.

If the horse fell, or if she were shaken free, she would be flung to instant death, or be fearfully bruised under the pounding hoofs of the big horse.

The young farmer's appreciation of the peril was instant; unused as he was to meeting such emergency, there was neither panic nor hesitancy in his actions.

He writhed farther out upon the limb of the leaning oak until he was direct above the road. The big bay naturally kept to the middle, for there was no obstruction in its path.

To have dropped to the highway would have put Hiram to instant disadvantage; for before he could have recovered himself after the drop the horse would have been upon him.

Now, swinging with both legs wrapped around the tough limb, and his left hand gripping a smaller branch, but with his back to the plunging brute, the youth glanced under his right armpit to judge the distance and the on-rush of the horse and its helpless rider.

He knew she saw him. Swift as was the steed's approach, Hiram had seen the change come into the expression of the girl's face.

"Clear your foot of the stirrup!" he shouted, hoping the girl would understand.

With a confusing thunder of hoofbeats the bay came on—was beneath him—had passed!

Hiram's right arm shot out, curved slightly, and as his fingers gripped her sleeve, the girl let go. She was whisked out of the saddle and the horse swept on without her.

The strain of the girl's slight weight upon his arm lasted but a moment, for Hiram let go with his feet, swung down, and dropped.

They alighted in the roadway with so slight a jar that he scarcely staggered, but set the girl down gently, and for the passing of a breath her body swayed against him, seeking support.

Then she sprang a little away, and they stood looking at each other—Hiram panting and flushed, the girl with wide-open eyes out of which the terror had not yet faded, and cheeks still colorless.

So they stood, for fully half a minute, speechless, while the thunder of the bay's hoofs passed further and further away and finally was lost in the distance.

And it wasn't excitement that kept the boy dumb; for that was all over, and he had been as cool as need be through the incident. But it was unbounded amazement that made him stare so at the slight girl confronting him.

He had seen her brilliant, dark little face before. Only once—but that one occasion had served to photograph her features on his memory.

For the second time he had been of service to her; but he knew instantly—and the fact did not puzzle him—that she did not recognize him.

It had been so dark in the unlighted side street back in Crawberry the evening of their first meeting that Hiram believed (and was glad) that neither she nor her father would recognize him as the boy who had kept their carriage from going into the open ditch.

And he had played rescuer again—and in a much more heroic manner. This was the daughter of the man whom he had thought to be a prosperous farmer, and whose card Hiram had lost.

He had hoped the gentleman might have a job for him; but now Hiram was not looking for a job. He had given himself heartily to the project of making the old Atterson farm pay; nor was he the sort of fellow to show fickleness in such a project.

Before either Hiram or the girl broke the silence—before that silence could become awkward, indeed—there started into hearing the ring of rapid hoofbeats again. But it was not the runaway returning.

The mate of the latter appeared, and he came jogging along the road, very much in hand, the rider seemingly quite unflurried.

This was a big, ungainly, beak-nosed boy, whose sleeves were much too short, and trousers-legs likewise, to hide Nature's abundant gift to him in the matter of bone and knuckle. He was freckled and wore a grin that was not even sheepish.

Somehow, this stolidity and inappreciation of the peril the girl had so recently escaped, made Hiram feel sudden indignation.

But the girl herself took the lout to task—before Hiram could say a word.

"I told you that horse could not bear the whip, Peter!" she exclaimed, with wrathful gaze. "How dared you strike him?"

"Aw—I only touched him up a bit," drawled the youth. "You said you could ride anything, didn't you?" and his grin grew wider. "But I see ye had to get off."

Here Hiram could stand it no longer, and he blurted out:

"She might have been killed! I believe that horse is running yet——"

"Well, why didn't you stop it?" demanded the other youth, "impudently. You had a chance."

"He saved me," cried the girl, looking at Hiram now with shining eyes. "I don't know how to thank him."

"He might have stopped the horse while he was about it," growled the fellow, picking up his own reins again. "Now I'll have to ride after it."

"You'd better," said the little lady, sharply. "If father knew that horse had run away with me he would be dreadfully put out. You hurry after him, Peter."

The lout never said a word in reply, but his horse carried him swiftly out of sight in the wake of the runaway. Then the girl turned again to Hiram and the young farmer knew that he was being keenly examined by her bright black eyes.

"I am very sure father will not keep him," declared the girl, looking at Hiram thoughtfully. "He is too careless—and I don't like him, anyway. Do you live around here?"

"I expect to," replied Hiram, smiling. "I have just come. I am going to stay at this next house, along the road."

"Oh! where the old gentleman died last week?"

"Yes. Mrs. Atterson was left the place by her uncle, and I am going to run it for her."

"Oh, dear! then you've got a place to work?" queried the little lady, with plain disappointment in her tone. "I am sure father would like to have you instead of Peter."

But Hiram shook his head slowly, though still smiling,

"I'm obliged to you," he said; "but I have agreed to stop with Mrs. Atterson for a time."

"I want father to meet you just the same," she declared.

She had a way about her that impressed Hiram with the idea that she seldom failed in getting what she wanted. If she was not a spoiled child, she certainly was a very much indulged one.

But she was pretty! Dark, petite, with a brilliant smile, flashing eyes, and a riot of blue-black curls, she was verily the daintiest and prettiest little creature the young farmer had ever seen.

"I am Lettie Bronson," she said, frankly. "I live down the road toward Scoville. We have only just come here."

"I know where you live," said Hiram, smiling and nodding.

"You must come and see us. I want you to know father. He's the very nicest man there is, I think."

"He came all the way East here so as to live near my school—I go to the St. Beris school in Scoville. It's awfully nice, and the girls are very fashionable; but I'd be too lonely to live if daddy wasn't right near me all the time.

"What is your name?" she asked suddenly.

Hiram told her.

"Why! that's a regular farmer's name, isn't it—Hiram?" and she laughed—a clear and sweet sound, that made an inquisitive squirrel that had been watching them scamper away to his hollow, chattering.

"I don't know about that," returned the young farmer, shaking his head and smiling. "I ought by good rights to be 'a worker in brass', according to the Bible. That was the trade of Hiram, of the tribe of Naphtali, who came out of Tyre to make all the brass work for Solomon's temple."

"Oh! and there was a King Hiram, of Tyre, too, wasn't there," cried Lettie, laughing. "You might be a king, you know."

"That seems to be an unprofitable trade now-a-days," returned the young fellow, shaking his head. "I think I will be the namesake of Hiram, the brass-smith, for it is said of him that he was 'filled with wisdom and understanding' and that is what I want to be if I am going to run Mrs. Atterson's farm and make it pay."

"You're a funny boy," said the girl, eyeing him furiously. "You're—you're not at all like Pete—or these other boys about Scoville."

"And that Pete Dickerson isn't any good at all! I shall tell daddy all about how he touched up that horse and made him run. Here he comes now!"

They had been walking steadily along the road toward the Atterson house, and in the direction the runaway had taken. Pete Dickerson appeared, riding one of the bays and leading the one that had been frightened.

The latter was all of a lather, was blowing hard, and before the horses reached them, Hiram saw that the runaway was in bad shape.

"Hold on!" he cried to the lout. "Breathe that horse a while. Let him stand. He ought to be rubbed down, too. Don't you see the shape he is in?"

"Aw, what's eatin' you?" demanded Pete, eyeing the speaker with much disfavor.

The horse, when he stopped, was trembling all over. His nostrils were dilated and as red as blood, and strings of foam were dripping from his bit.

"Don't let him stand there in the shade," spoke Hiram, more "mildly. He'll take a chill. Here! let me have him."

He approached the still frightened horse, and Pete jerked the bridle-rein. The horse started back and snorted.

"Stand 'round there, ye 'tarnal nuisance!" exclaimed Pete.

But Hiram caught the bridle and snatched it from the other fellow's hand.

"Just let me manage him a minute," said Hiram, leading the horse into the sunshine.

He patted him, and soothed him, and the horse ceased trembling and his ears pricked up. Hiram, still keeping the reins in his hand, loosened the cinches and eased the saddle so that the animal could breathe better.

There were bunches of dried sage-grass growing by the roadside, and the young farmer tore off a couple of these bunches and used them to wipe down the horse's legs. Pretty soon the creature forgot his fright and looked like a normal horse again.

"If he was mine I'd give him whip a-plenty—till he learned better," drawled Pete Dickerson, finally.

"Don't you ever dare touch him with the whip again!" cried the girl, stamping her foot. "He will not stand it. You were told——"

"Aw, well," said the fellow, "'I didn't think he was going to cut up as bad as that. These Western horses ain't more'n half broke, anyway."

"I think he is perfectly safe for you to ride now, Miss Bronson," said Hiram, quietly. "I'll give you a hand up. But walk him home, please."

He had tightened the cinches again. Lettie put her tiny booted foot in his hand (she wore a very pretty dark green habit) and with perfect ease the young farmer lifted her into the saddle.

"Good-bye—and thank you again!" she said, softly, giving him her free hand just as the horse started.

"Say! you're the fellow who's going to live at Atterson's place?" observed Pete. "I'll see you later," and he waved his hand airily as he rode off.

"So that's Pete Dickerson, is it?" ruminated Hiram, as he watched the horses out of sight. "Well, if his father, Sam, is anything like him, we certainly have got a sweet pair of neighbors!"

CHAPTER XII
SOMETHING ABOUT A PASTURE FENCE

That afternoon Hiram hitched up the old horse and drove into town

He went to see the lawyer who had transacted Uncle Jeptha Atterson's small business in the old man's lifetime, and had made his will—Mr. Strickland. Hiram judged that this gentleman would know as much about the Atterson place as anybody.

"No—Mr. Atterson never said anything to me about giving a neighbor water-rights," the lawyer said. "Indeed, Mr. Atterson was not a man likely to give anything away—until he had got through with it himself.

"Dickerson once tried to buy a right at that corner of the Atterson pasture; but he and the old gentleman couldn't come to terms.

"Dickerson has no water on his place, saving his well and his rights on the river. It makes it bad for him, I suppose; but I do not advise Mrs. Atterson to let that fence stand. Give that sort of a man an inch and he'll take a mile."

"But what shall I do?"

"That's professional advice, young man," returned the lawyer, "smiling. But I will give it to you without charge.

"Merely go and pull the new posts up and replace them on the line. If Dickerson interferes with you, come to me and we'll have him bound over before the Justice of the Peace.

"You represent Mrs. Atterson and are within her rights. That's the best I can tell you."

Now, Hiram was not desirous of starting any trouble—legal or otherwise—with a neighbor; but neither did he wish to see anybody take advantage of his old boarding mistress. He knew that, beside farming for her, he would probably have to defend her from many petty annoyances like the present case.

So he bought the wire he needed for repairs, a few other things that were necessary, and drove back to the farm, determined to go right ahead and await the consequences.

Among his purchases was an axe. In the workshop on the farm was a fairly good grindstone; only the treadle was broken and Hiram had to repair this before he could make much headway in grinding the axe. Henry Pollock lived too far away to be called upon in such a small emergency.

Being obliged to work alone sharpens one's wits. The young farmer had to resort to shifts and expedients on every hand, as he went along.

The day before, while wandering in the wood, he had marked several white oaks of the right size for posts. He would have preferred cedars, of course; but those trees were scarce on the Atterson tract—and they might be needed for some more important job later on.

When he came up to the house at noon to feed the stock and make his own frugal meal in the farm house kitchen, the posts were cut. After dinner he harnessed the horse to the farm wagon, and went down for the posts, taking the rolls of wire along to drop beside the fence.

The horse was a steady, willing creature, and seemed to have no tricks. He did not drive very well on the road, of course; but that wasn't what they needed a horse for.

Driving was a secondary matter.

Hiram loaded his posts and hauled them to the pasture, driving inside the fence line and dropping a post wherever one had rotted out.

Yet posts that had rotted at the ground were not so easy to draw out, as the young farmer very well knew, and he set his wits to work to make the removal of the old posts easy of accomplishment.

He found an old, but strong, carpenter's horse in the shed, to act as a fulcrum, and a seasoned bar of hickory as a lever. There was never an old farm yet that didn't have a useful heap of junk, and Hiram had already scratched over Uncle Jeptha's collection of many years' standng.

He found what he sought in a wrought iron band some half inch in thickness with a heavy hook attached to it by a single strong link. He fitted this band upon the larger end of the hickory bar, wedging it tightly into place.

A short length of trace chain completed his simple post-puller. And he could easily carry the outfit from place to place as it was needed.

When he found a weak or rotting post, he pulled the staples that held the strands of wire to it and and then set the trestle alongside the post. Resting the lever on the trestle, he dropped the end link of the chain on the hook, looped the chain around the post, and hooked on with another link. Bearing down on the lever brought the post out of the ground every time.

With a long-handled spade Hiram cleaned out the old holes, or enlarged them, and set his new posts, one after the other. He left the wires to be tightened and stapled later.

It was not until the next afternoon that he worked down as far as the water-hole. Meanwhile he had seen nothing of the neighbors and neither knew, nor cared, whether they were watching him or not.

But it was evident that the Dickersons had kept tabs on the young farmer's progress, for, he had no more than pulled the posts out of the water-hole and started to reset them on the proper line, than the long-legged Pete Dickerson appeared.

"Hey, you!" shouted Pete. "What are you monkeying with that line fence for?"

"Because I won't have time to fix it later," responded Hiram, calmly.

"Fresh Ike, ain't yer?" demanded young Dickerson.

He was half a head taller than Hiram, and plainly felt himself safe in adopting bullying tactics.

"You put them posts back where you found 'em and string the wires again in a hurry—or I'll make yer."

"This is Mrs. Atterson's fence," said Hiram, quietly. "I have made inquiries about the line, and I know where it belongs."

"No part of this water-hole belongs on your side of the fence, Dickerson, and as long as I represent Mrs. Atterson it's not going to be grabbed."

"Say! the old man gave my father the right to a part of this hole long ago."

"Show your legal paper to that effect," promptly suggested Hiram. "Then we will let it stand until the lawyers decide the matter."

Pete was silent for a minute; meanwhile Hiram continued to dig his hole, and finally set the first post into place.

"I tell you to take that post out o' there, Mister," exclaimed Pete, suddenly approaching the other. "I don't like you, anyway. You helped git me turned off up there to Bronson's yesterday. If you wouldn't have put your fresh mouth in about the horse that gal wouldn't have knowed so much to tell her father. Now you stop foolin' with this fence or I'll lick you."

Hiram Strong's disposition was far from being quarrelsome. He only laughed at first and said:

"Why, that won't do you any good in the end, Peter. Thrashing me won't give you and your father the right to usurp rights at this water-hole.

"There was very good reason, as I can see, for old Mr. Atterson refusing to let you water your stock here. In time of drouth the branch probably furnished no more water than his own cattle needed. And it will be the same with my employer."

"You'd better have less talk about it, and set back them posts," declared Pete, decidedly, laying off his coat and pulling up his shirt sleeves.

"I hope you won't try anything foolish, Peter," said Hiram, resting on his shovel handle.

"Huh!" grunted Pete, eyeing him sideways as might an evil-disposed dog.

"We're not well matched," observed Hiram, quietly, "and whether you thrashed me, or I thrashed you, nothing would be proved by it in regard to the line fence."

"I'll show you what I can prove!" cried Pete, and rushed for him.

In a catch-as-catch-can wrestle Pete Dickerson might have been able to overturn Hiram Strong. But the latter did not propose to give the long-armed youth that advantage.

He dropped the spade, stepped nimbly aside, and as Pete lunged past him the young farmer doubled his fist and struck his antagonist solidly under the ear.

That was the only blow struck—that and the one when Pete struck the ground. The bigger fellow rolled over, grunted, and gazed up at Hiram with amazement struggling with the rage expressed in his features.

"I told you we were not well matched, Peter," spoke Hiram, calmly. "Why fight about it? You have no right on your side, and I do not propose to see Mrs. Atterson robbed of this water privilege."

Pete climbed to his feet slowly, and picked up his coat. He felt of his neck carefully and then looked at his hand, with the idea evidently that such a heavy blow must have brought blood. But of course there was none.

"I'll tell my dad—that's what I'll do," ejaculated the bully, at length, and he started immediately across the field, his long legs working like a pair of tongs in his haste to get over the ground.

But Hiram completed the setting of the posts at the water-hole without hearing further from any member of the Dickerson family.

CHAPTER XIII
THE UPROOTING

These early Spring days were busy ones for Hiram Strong. The mornings were frosty and he could not get to his fencing work until midforenoon. But there were plenty of other tasks ready to his hand.

There were two south windows in the farmhouse kitchen. He tried to keep some fire in the stove there day and night, sleeping as he did in Uncle Jeptha's old bedroom nearby.

Before these two windows he erected wide shelves and on these he set shallow boxes of rich earth which he had prepared under the cart shed. There was no frost under there, the earth was dry and the hens had scratched in it during the winter, so Hiram got all the well-sifted earth he needed for his seed boxes.

He used a very little commercial fertilizer in each box, and planted some of the seeds he had bought in Crawberry at an agricultural warehouse on Main Street.

Mrs. Atterson had expressed the hope that he would put in a variety of vegetables for their own use, and Hiram had followed her wishes. When the earth in the boxes had warmed up for several days he put in the long-germinating seeds, like tomato, onions, the salads, leek, celery, pepper, eggplant, and some beet seed to transplant for the early garden. It was too early yet to put in cabbage and cauliflower.

These boxes caught the sun for a good part of the day. In the afternoon when the sun had gone, Hiram covered the boxes with old quilts and did not uncover them again until the sun shone in the next morning. He had decided to start his early plants in this way because he hadn't the time at present to build frames outside.

During the early mornings and late afternoons, too, he began to make the small repairs around the house and outbuildings. Hiram was handy with tools; indeed, a true farmer should be a good mechanic as well. He must often combine carpentry and wheelwrighting and work at the forge, with his agricultural pursuits. Hiram was something better than a "cold-iron blacksmith."

When it came to stretching the wire of the pasture fence he had to resort to his inventive powers. There are plenty of wire stretchers that can be purchased; but they cost money.

The young farmer knew that Mrs. Atterson had no money to waste, and he worked for her just as he would have worked for himself.

One man working alone cannot easily stretch wire and make a good job of it without some mechanism to help him. Hiram's was simple and easily made.

A twelve-inch section of perfectly round post, seven or eight inches through, served as the drum around which to wind the wire, and two twenty-penny nails driven into the side of the drum, close together, were sufficient to prevent the wire from slipping.

To either end of the drum Hiram passed two lengths of Number 9 wire through large screweyes, making a double loop into which the hook of a light timber chain would easily catch. Into one end of the drum he drove a headless spike, upon which the hand-crank of the grindstone fitted, and was wedged tight.

In using this ingenious wire stretcher, he stapled his wire to post number one, carried the length past post number two, looped the chain around post number three, having the chain long enough so that he might tauten the wire and hold the crankhandle steady with his knee or left arm while he drove the holding staple in post number two. And so repeat, ad infinitum.

After he had made this wire-stretcher the young fellow got along famously upon his fencing and could soon turn his attention to other matters, knowing that the cattle would be perfectly safe in the pasture for the coming season.

The old posts he collected on the wagon and drew into the dooryard, piling them beside the woodshed. There was not an overabundant supply of firewood cut and Hiram realized that Mrs. Atterson would use considerable in her kitchen stove before the next winter, even if she did not run a sitting room fire for long this spring.

Using a bucksaw is not only a thankless job at any time, but it is no saving of time or money. There was a good two-handed saw in the shed and Hiram found a good rat-tail file. With the aid of a home-made saw-holder and a monkey wrench he sharpened and set this saw and then got Henry Pollock to help him for a day.

Henry wasn't afraid of work, and the two boys sawed and split the old and well-seasoned posts, and some other wood, so that Hiram was enabled to pile several tiers of stove-wood under the shed against the coming of Mrs. Atterson to her farm.

"If the season wasn't so far advanced, I could cut a lot of wood, draw it up, and hire a gasoline engine and saw to come on the place and saw us enough to last a year. I'll do that next winter," Hiram said.

"That's what we all ought to do," agreed his friend.

Henry Pollock was an observing farmer's boy and through him Hiram gained many pointers as to the way the farmers in that locality put in their crops and cultivated them.

He learned, too, through Henry who was supposed to be the best farmer in the neighborhood, who had special success with certain crops, and who had raised the best seedcorn in the locality.

It was not particularly a trucking community; although, since Scoville had begun to grow so fast and many city people had moved into that pleasant town, the local demand for garden produce had increased.

"It used to be a saying here," said Henry, "that a bushel of winter turnips would supply all the needs of Scoville. But that ain't exactly so now.

"The stores all want green stuff in season, and are beginning to pay cash for truck instead of only offering to exchange groceries for the stuff we raise. I guess if a man understood truck raising he could make something in this market."

Hiram decided that this was so, on looking over the marketing possibilities of Scoville.

There was a canning factory which put up string beans, corn, and tomatoes; but the prices per hundred-weight for these commodities did not encourage Hiram to advise Mrs. Atterson to try and raise anything for the canneries. A profit could not be made out of such crops on a one-horse farm.

For instance, the neighboring farmers did not plant their tomato seeds until it was pretty safe to do so in the open ground. The cannery did not want the tomato pack to come on until late in August. By that time the cream of the prices for garden-grown tomatoes had been skimmed by the early truckers.

The same with sweet corn and green beans. The cannery demanded these vegetables at so late a date that the market-price was generally low.

These facts Hiram bore in mind as he planned his season's work, and especially the kitchen garden. This latter he planned to be about two acres in extent—rather a large plot, but he proposed to set his rows of almost every vegetable far enough apart to be worked with a horse cultivator.

Some crops—for instance onions, carrots, and other "fine stuff"—must be weeded by hand to an extent, and if the soil is rich enough rows twelve or fifteen inches apart show better results.

Between such rows a wheelhoe can be used to good advantage, and that was one tool—with a seed-sowing combination—that Hiram had told Mrs. Atterson she must buy if he was to practically attend to the whole farm for her. Hand-hoeing, in both field and garden crops, is antediluvian.

Thus, during this week and a half of preparation, Hiram made ready for the uprooting of Mrs. Atterson from the boarding house in Crawberry to the farm some distance out of Scoville.

The good lady had but one wagon load of goods to be transferred from her old quarters to the new home. Many of the articles she brought were heirlooms which she had stored in the boarding house cellar, or articles associated with her happy married life, which had been shortened by her husband's death when he was comparatively a young man.

These Mrs. Atterson saw piled on the wagon early on Saturday morning, and she had insisted upon climbing upon the seat beside the driver herself and riding with him all the way.

The boarders gathered on the steps to see her go. The two spinster ladies had already taken possession, and had served breakfast to the disgruntled members of Mother Atterson's family.

"You'll be back again," prophesied Mr. Crackit, shaking the old lady by the hand. "And when you do, just let me know. I'll come and board with you."

"I wouldn't have you in my house again, Fred Crackit, for two farms," declared the ex-boarding house keeper, with asperity.

"I hope you told these people about my hot water, Mrs. Atterson," creaked Mr. Peebles, from the step, where he stood muffled in a shawl because of the raw morning air.

"If I didn't you can tell 'em yourself," returned she, with satisfaction.

And so it went—the good-byes of these unappreciative boarders selfish to the last! Mother Atterson sighed—a long, happy, and satisfying sigh—when the lumbering wagon turned the first corner.

"Thanks be!" she murmured. "I sha'n't care if they don't have a driblet of gravy at supper tonight."

Then she shook herself and stared straight ahead. On the very next corner—she had insisted that none of the other people at the house should observe their flitting—stood two figures, both forlorn.

Old Lem Camp, with a lean suit-case at his feet, and Sister with a bulging carpetbag which she had brought with her months before from the charity institution, and into which she had stuffed everything she owned in the world.

Their faces brightened perceptibly when they beheld Mrs. Atterson perched high beside the driver on the load of furniture and bedding. The driver drew in his span of big horses and the wheels grated against the curb.

"You climb right in behind, Mr. Camp," said the good lady. "There's room for you up under the canvas top—and I had him spread a mattress so't you can take it easy all the way, if you like.

"Sister, you scramble up here and sit in betwixt me and this man. And do look out—you're spillin' things out o' that bag like it was a Christmas cornucopia. Come on, now! Toss it behind us, onto them other things. There! we'll go on—and no more stops, I hope, till we reach the farm."

But that couldn't be. It was a long drive, and the man was good to his team. He rested them at the top of every hill, and sometimes at the bottom. They had to stop two hours for dinner and to "breathe 'em," as the man said.

At that time Mother Atterson produced a goodsized market basket— her familiar companion when she had hunted bargains in the city—and it was filled with sandwiches, and pickles, and crackers, and cookies, and a whole boiled fowl (fowl were cheaper and more satisfying than the scrawny chickens then in market) and hard-boiled eggs, and cheese, with numbers of other less important eatables tucked into corners of the basket to "wedge" the larger packages of food.

The four picnicked in the sun, with the furniture wagon to break the keen wind, passing around hot coffee in a can, from hand to hand, the driver having built a campfire to heat the coffee beside the country road.

But after that stop—for they were well into the country now—there was no keeping Sister on the wagon-seat. She had learned to drop down and mount again as lively as a cricket.

She tore along the edge of the road, with her hair flying, and her hat hanging by its ribbons. She chased a rabbit, and squirrels, and picked certain green branches, and managed to get her hands and the front of her dress all "stuck up" with spruce gum in trying to get a piece big enough to chew.

"Drat the young'un!" exclaimed Mother Atterson. "I can see plainly I'd never ought to brought her, but should have sent her back to the institution. She'll be as wild as Mr. March's hare—whoever he was—out here in the country."

But Old Lem Camp gave her no trouble. He effaced himself just as he had at the boarding house supper table. He seldom spoke—never unless he was spoken to; and he lay up under the roof of the furniture wagon, whether asleep, or no, Mrs. Atterson could not tell.

"He's as odd as Dick's hat-band," the ex-boarding house mistress confided to the driver. "But, bless you! the easiest critter to get along with—you never saw his beat. If I'd a house full of Lem Camps to cook for, I'd think I was next door to heaven."

It was dusk when they arrived in sight of the little house beside the road in which Uncle Jeptha Atterson had lived out his long life. Hiram had a good fire going in both the kitchen and sitting room, and the lamplight flung through the windows made the place look cheerful indeed to the travelers.

"My soul and body!" croaked the good lady, when she got down from the wagon and Hiram caught her in his arms to save her from a fall. "I'm as stiff as a poker—and that's a fact. But I'm glad to get here."

Hiram's amazement when he saw Sister and Old Lem Camp was only expressed in his look. He said nothing. The driver of the wagon backed it to the porch step and then took out his team and, with Hiram's help, led them to the stable, fed them, and bedded them down for the night. He was to sleep in one of the spare beds and go back to town the following day.

Mother Atterson took off her best dress, slipped into a familiar old gingham and bustled around the kitchen as naturally as though she had been there all her life.

She fried ham and eggs, and made biscuit, and opened a couple of tins of peaches she had brought, and finally set before them a repast satisfying if not dainty, and seasoned with a cheerful spirit at least.

"I vum!" she exclaimed, sitting down for the first time in years "at the first table." "If this don't beat Crawberry and them boarders, I'm crazy as a loon. Pour the coffee, Sister—and don't be stingy with the milk. Milk's only five cents a quart here, and it's eight in town. But, gracious, child! sugar don't cost no less."

Old Lem Camp sat beside Hiram, as he had at the boarding-house table. He had scarcely spoken since his arrival; but now, under cover of the talk of Mother Atterson, the driver of the furniture van, and Sister, he began one of his old-time monologues:

"Old, old—nothing to look forward to—then the prospect opens up—just like light breaking through the clouds after a storm—let's see; I want a piece of bread—bread's on Sister's side—I can reach it—hum! no Crackit to-night—fool jokes—silly fellow—ah! the butter—Where's the butterknife?—Sister's forgotten the butter-knife—no! here 'tis—That woman's an angel—nothing less—an angel in a last season's bonnet and a shabby gown—Hah! practical angels couldn't use wings—they'd be in the way in the kitchen—ham and eggs—gravy—fit for gods to eat—and not to worry again where next week's victuals are to come from!"

Hiram noted all the old mail said, and the last phrase enlightened him immensely as to why Old Lem Camp was so "queer." That was the trouble on the old man's mind—the trouble that had stifled him, and made him appear "half cracked" as the boarding-house jester and Peebles had said.

Lem Camp, too old to ever get another job in the city, had for five years been worrying from day to day about his bare existence. And evidently he saw that bogie of the superannuated disappearing in the distance.

After the truck driver had gone to bed, and Camp himself, and Sister had fallen asleep over the last of the dish-wiping, Mother Atterson confided in Hiram, to a degree.

"Now, this gal can be made useful. She can help me in the house, and she can help outside, too.

"She's a poor, unfortunate creature—I know and humbly is no name for her looks! But mebbe we can send her to the school nearby, and she ought to get some color in her face if she's out o' doors some—and some flesh on her skinny body.

"I don't know as I could get along without Sister," ruminated Mother Atterson, shaking her head.

"And as for Lem Camp—bless you! he won't eat more'n a fly, and who else would give him houseroom? Why, Hiram, I just had to bring him with me. If I hadn't, I'd felt just as conscience-stricken as though I'd moved and left a cat behind in an empty house!"

CHAPTER XIV
GETTING IN THE EARLY CROPS

Mother Atterson had breakfast the next morning by lamplight, because the truckman wanted to make an early start.

Hiram had already begun early rising, however, for the farmer who does not get up before the sun in the spring needs must do his chores at night by lantern-light. The eight-hour law can never be a rule on the farm.

But Sister was up, too, and out of the house, running as wild as a rabbit. Hiram caught her in the barnyard trying to clamber on the cow's back to ride her about the enclosure. Sister was afraid of nothing that lived and walked, having all the courage of ignorance.

She found that she could not in safety clamber over the pig-lot fence and catch one of the shoats. Old Mother Hog ran at her with open mouth and Sister came back from that expedition with a torn frock and some new experience.

"I never knew anything so fat could run," she confided to Hiram. "Old Missus Poundly, who lived on our block, and weighed three hundred pounds, couldn't run, I bet!"

Mr. Camp was not disturbed by Mrs. Atterson, but was allowed to sleep as long as he liked, while she kept a little breakfast hot for him and the coffeepot on the back of the stove.

The old lady became interested at once in all Hiram had done toward beginning the spring work. She learned about the seed in the window boxes (some of them were already breaking the soil) about watering them and covering them properly and immediately took those duties off Hiram's hands.

"If Sister an' me can't do the light chores around this place and leave you to 'tend to the bigger things, then we ain't no good and had better go back to the boarding house," she announced.

"Oh, Mis' Atterson! You wouldn't go back to town, would you?" pleaded Sister. "Why, there's real hens—and a cow that will give milk bimeby, Hi says—and a horse that wiggles his ears and talks right out loud when he's hungry, for I heard him—and pigs that squeal and run, an' they're jest as fat as butter——"

"Well, to stay here we've all got to work, Sister," declared her mistress. "So get at them dishes now and be quick about it. There's forty times more chores to do here than there was back in Crawberry—But, thanks be! there ain't no gravy to worry about."

"And there ain't no boarders to make fun of me," said Sister, thoughtfully. Then, she announced, after some rumination: "I like pigs better than I do boarders Mis' Atterson."

"Well, I should think you would!" exclaimed that lady, tartly. "Pigs has got some sense."

Hiram laughed at this. "You'll find the pigs demanding gravy, just the same—and very urgent about it they are, too," he told them.

But he was glad to give the small chores over into their hands, and went to work immediately to prepare for putting in the early crops.

He had already cleared the rubbish off the piece of ground selected for the garden, and had burned it. He hauled out stable manure from the barnyard and gave an acre and a half of this piece of land a good dressing.

The other half-acre was for early potatoes, and he wished to put the manure in the furrow for them, so did not top dress that strip of land. The frost was pretty well out of the ground by now; but even if some remained, plowing this high, well-drained piece would do no harm. Beside, Hiram was eager to get in early crops.

It was a still, hazy morning when he geared the old horse to the plow and headed him into the garden piece. He had determined to plow the entire plot at once, and instead of plowing "around and around" had paced off his lands and started in the middle, plowing "gee" instead of "haw".

This system is a bit more particular, and hard for the careless plowman; but it overcomes that unsightly "dead-furrow" in the middle of a field and brings the "finishing-furrow" on the edge. This insures better surface drainage and is a more scientific method of tillage.

The plow was rusty and the point was not in the very best condition; but after the first few rounds the share was cleaned off, and it began to slip through the moist earth and roll it over in a long, brown ribbon behind him.

Hiram Strong clung to the plow handles, a rope-rein in each hand, and watched the plow and the horse and the land ahead with an eye as keen as that of a river-pilot.

As the strip of turned earth grew wider and longer Sister ran out to see him work. She watched the plow turn the mulch into the furrow and lay the brown, greasy mold upon it, with wide-open eyes.

"Why!" cried she, "wouldn't it be nice if we could go right along with a plow and bury our past like that—cover everything mean and nasty up, and forget it! That institution they put me in—and the old woman I lived with before that, who drank so much gin and beat me—and the boarders—and that boy who used to pull my braids whenever he met me—My that would be fine!"

"I reckon that is what Life does do for us," returned Hiram, thoughtfully, stopping at the end of the furrow to mop his brow and let the old horse breathe. "Yes, sir! Life plows all the experience under, and it ought to enrich our future existence, just as this stuff I'm plowing under here will decay and enrich the soil."

"But the plow don't turn it quite under in spots," said Sister, with a sigh. "Leastways, I can't help remembering the bad things once in a while."

There were certain other individuals who found out very soon that Hiram was plowing, too. Those were the hens. There were not more than fifteen or twenty of the scrubby creatures, and they began to follow the plow and pick up grubs and worms.

"I tell you one thing that I've got to do before we put in much," Hiram told the ex-boarding house mistress at noon.

"What's that, Hi? Don't go very deep down into my pocket, for it won't stand it. After paying my bills, and paying for moving out here, I ain't got much money left—and that's a fact!"

"It won't cost much, but we've got to have a yard for the hens. Hens and a garden will never mix successfully. Unless you enclose them you might as well have no garden in that spot where I'm plowing."

"There warn't but five eggs to-day," said Mrs. Atterson. "Mebbe we'd better chop the heads off 'em, one after the other, and eat 'em."

"They'll lay better as it grows warmer. That henhouse must be fixed before next winter. It's too draughty," said Hi. "And then, hens can't lay well—especially through the winter—if they haven't the proper kind of food."

"But three or four of the dratted things want to stay on the nest all the time," complained the old lady.

"If I was you, Mrs. Atterson," Hiram said, soberly, "I'd spend five dollars for a hundred eggs of well-bred stock.

"I'd set these hens as fast as they get broody, and raise a decent flock of biddies for next year. Scrub hens are just as bad as scrub cows. The scrubs will eat quite as much as full-bloods, yet the returns from the scrubs are much less."

"I declare!" exclaimed Mrs. Atterson, "a hen's always been just a hen to me—one's the same as another, exceptin' the feathers on some is prettier."

"To-night I'll show you some breeders' catalogs and you can think the matter over as to what kind of a fowl you want," said the young farmer.

He went back to his job after dinner and kept steadily at work until three o'clock before there came a break. Then he saw a carriage drive into the yard, and a few moments later a man In a long gray coat came striding across the lot toward him.

Hiram knew the gentleman at once—it was Mr. Bronson, the father of the girl he had saved from the runaway. To tell the truth, the boy had rather wondered about his non-appearance during the days that had elapsed. But now he came with hand held out, and his first words explained the seeming omission:

"I've been away for more than a week, my boy, or I should have seen you before. You're Hiram Strong, aren't you—the boy my little girl has been talking so much about?"

"I don't know how much Miss Lettie has been talking about me," laughed Hiram. "Full and plenty, I expect."

"And small blame to her," declared Mr. Bronson. "I won't waste time telling you how grateful I am. I had just time to turn that boy of Dickerson's off before I was called away. Now, my lad, I want you to come and work for me."

"Why, much as I might like to, sir, I couldn't do that," said Hiram.

"Now, now! we'll fix it somehow. Lettie has set her heart on having you around the place.

"You're the second young man I've been after whom I was sure would suit me, since we moved on to the old Fleigler place. The first fellow I can't find; but don't tell me that I am going to be disappointed in you, too."

"Mr. Bronson," said Hiram, gravely, "I'm sorry to say 'No.' A little while ago I'd have been delighted to take up with any fair offer you might have made me. But I have agreed with Mrs. Atterson to run her place for two seasons."

"Two years!" exclaimed Mr. Bronson.

"Yes, sir. Practically. I must put her on her feet and make the old farm show a profit."

"You're pretty young to take such responsibility upon your shoulders, are you not?" queried the gentleman, eyeing him curiously.

"I'm seventeen. I began to work with my father as soon as I could lift a hoe. I love farm work. And I've passed my word to stick to Mrs. Atterson."

"That's the old lady up to the house?"

"Yes, sir."

"But she wouldn't hold you to your bargain if she saw you could better yourself, would she?"

"She would not have to," Hiram said, firmly, and he began to feel a little disappointed in his caller. "A bargain's a bargain—there's no backing out of it."

"But suppose I should make it worth her while to give you up?" pursued Mr. Bronson. "I'll sound her a bit, eh? I tell you that Lettie has set her heart on having you, as we cannot find another chap whom we were looking for."

Now, Hiram knew that this referred to him; but he said nothing. Besides, he did not feel too greatly pleased that the strongest reason for Mr. Bronson's wishing to hire him was his little daughter's demand. It was just a fancy of Miss Lettie's. And another day, she might have the fancy to turn him off.

"No, sir," spoke Hiram, more firmly. "It is useless. I am obliged to you; but I must stick by Mrs. Atterson."

"Well, my lad," said the Westerner, putting out his hand again. "I am glad to see you know how to keep a promise, even if it isn't to your advantage. And I am grateful to you for turning that trick for my little girl the other day."

"I hope you'll come over and see us—and I shall watch your work here. Most of these fellows around here are pretty slovenly farmers in my estimation; I hope you will do better than the average."

He went back across the field and Hiram returned to his plowing. The young farmer saw the bay horses driven slowly out of the yard and along the road.

He saw the flutter of a scarf from the carriage and knew that Lettie Bronson was with her father; but she did not look out at him as he toiled behind the old horse in the furrow.

However, there was no feeling of disappointment in Hiram Strong's mind—and this fact somewhat surprised him. He had been so attracted by the girl, and had wished in the beginning so much to be engaged by Mr. Bronson, that he had considered it a mighty disappointment when he had lost the Westerner's card.

However, his apathy in the matter was easily explained. He had taken hold of the work on the Atterson place. His plans were growing in his mind for the campaign before him. His interest was fastened upon the contract he had made with the old lady.

His hand was, literally now, "to the plow"—and he was not looking back.

He finished the piece that day, and likewise drew out some lime that he had bought at Scoville and spread it broadcast upon all the garden patch save that in which he intended to put potatoes.

Although it is an exploded doctrine that the application of lime to potato ground causes scab, it is a fact that it will aid in spreading the disease. Hiram was sure enough—because of the sheep-sorrel on the piece—that it all needed sweetening, but he decided against the lime at this time.

As soon as Hiram had drag-harrowed the piece he laid off two rows down the far end, as being less tempting to the straying hens, and planted early peas—the round-seeded variety, hardier than the wrinkled kinds. These pea-rows were thirty inches apart, and he dropped the peas by hand and planted them very thickly.

It doesn't pay to be niggardly with seed in putting in early peas, at any rate—the thicker they come up the better, and in these low bush varieties the thickly growing vines help support each other.

This garden piece—almost two acres—was oblong in shape. An acre is just about seventy paces square. Hiram's garden was seventy by a hundred and forty paces, or thereabout.

Therefore, the young farmer had two seventy-yard rows of peas, or over four hundred feet of drill. He planted two quarts of peas at a cost of seventy cents.

With ordinary fortune the crop should be much more than sufficient for the needs of the house while the peas were in a green state, for being a quick growing vegetable, they are soon past.

Hiram, however, proposed putting in a surplus of almost everything he planted in this big garden—especially of the early vegetables—for he believed that there would be a market for them in Scoville.

The ground was very cold yet, and snow flurries swept over the field every few days; but the peas were under cover and were off his mind; Hiram knew they would be ready to pop up above the surface just as soon as the warm weather came in earnest, and peas do not easily rot in the ground.

In two weeks, or when the weather was settled, he proposed planting other kinds of peas alongside these first two rows, so as to have a succession up to mid-summer.

Next the young farmer laid off his furrows for early potatoes. He had bought a sack of an extra-early variety, yet a potato that, if left in the ground the full length of the season, would make a good winter variety—a "long keeper."

His potato rows he planned to have three feet apart, and he plowed the furrows twice, so as to have them clean and deep.

Henry Pollock happened to come by while he was doing this, and stopped to talk and watch Hiram. To tell the truth, Henry and his folks were more than a little interested in what the young farmer would do with the Atterson place.

Like other neighbors they doubted if the stranger knew as much about the practical work of farming as he claimed to know. "That feller from the city," the neighbors called Hiram behind his back, and that is an expression that completely condemns a man in the mind of the average countryman.

"What yer bein' so particular with them furrers for, Hiram?" asked Henry.

"If a job's worth doing at all, it's worth doing well, isn't it?" laughed the young farmer.

"We spread our manure broadcast—when we use any at all—for potatoes," said Henry, slowly. "Dad says if manure comes in contact with potatoes, they are apt to rot."

"That seems to be a general opinion," replied Hiram. "And it may be so under certain conditions. For that reason I am going to make sure that not much of this fertilizer comes in direct contact with my seed."

"How'll you do that?" "I'll show you," said Hiram.

Having run out his rows and covered the bottom of each furrow several inches deep with the manure, he ran his plow down one side of each furrow and turned the soil back upon the fertilizer, covering it and leaving a well pulverized seed bed for the potatoes to lie in.

"Well," said Henry, "that's a good wrinkle, too."

Hiram had purchased some formalin, mixed it with water according to the Government expert's instructions, and from time to time soaked his seed potatoes two hours in the antiseptic bath. In the evening he brought them into the kitchen and they all—even Old Lem Camp—cut up the potatoes, leaving two or three good eyes in each piece.

"I'd ruther do this than peel 'em for the boarders," remarked Sister, looking at her deeply-stained fingers reflectively. "And then, nobody won't say nothin' about my hands to me when I'm passin' dishes at the table."

The following day she helped Hiram drop the seed, and by night he had covered them by running his plow down the other side of the row and then smoothed the potato plat with a home-made "board" in lieu of a land-roller.

It was the twentieth of March, and not a farmer in the locality had yet put in either potatoes, or peas. Some had not as yet plowed for early potatoes, and Henry Pollock warned Hiram that he was "rushing the season."

"That may be," declared the young farmer to Mrs. Atterson. "But I believe the risk is worth taking. If we do get 'em good, we'll get 'em early and skim the cream of the local market. Now, you see!"

CHAPTER XV
TROUBLE BREWS

"Old Lem Camp," as he had been called for so many years that there seemed no disrespect in the title, was waking up. Not many mornings was he a lie-abed. And the lines in his forehead seemed to be smoothing out, and his eyes had lost something of their dullness.

It was true that, at first, he wandered about the farmstead muttering to himself in his old way—an endless monologue which was a jumble of comment, gratitude, and the brief memories of other days. It took some time to adjust his poor mind to the fact that he had no longer to fear that Poverty which had stalked ever before him like a threatening spirit.

Gratitude spurred him to the use of his hands. He was not a broken man—not bodily. Many light tasks soon fell to his share, and Mrs. Atterson told Hiram and Sister to let him do what he would. To busy himself would be the best thing in the world for the old fellow.

"That's what's been the matter with Mr. Camp for years," she declared, with conviction. "Because he passed the sixty-year mark, and it was against the practise of the paper company to keep employees on the payroll over that age, they turned Lem Camp off.

"Ridiculous! He was just as well able to do the tasks that he had learned to do mechanically as he had been any time for the previous twenty years. He had worked in that office forty years, and more, you understand.

"That's the worst thing about a corporation of that kind—it has no thought beyond its 'rules.' Old Mr. Bundy remembered Lem—that's all. If he hadn't so much stock in the concern they'd turn him off, too. I expect he knows it and that's what softened his heart to Old Lem.

"Now, let Lem take hold of whatever he can do, and git interested in it," declared the practical Mrs. Atterson, "and he'll show you that there's work left in him yet. Yes-sir-ree-sir! And if he'll work in the open air, all the better for him."

There was plenty for everybody to do, and Hiram would not say the old man nay. The seed boxes needed a good deal of attention, for they were to be lifted out into the air on warm days, and placed in the sun. And Old Lem could do this—and stir the soil in them, and pull out the grass and other weeds that started.

Hiram had planted early cabbage and cauliflower and egg-plant in other boxes, and the beets were almost big enough to transplant to the open ground. Beets are hardy and although hair-roots are apt to form on transplanted garden beets, the transplanting aids the growth in other ways and Hiram expected to have table-beets very early.

In the garden itself he had already run out two rows of later beets, the width of the plot. Bunched beets will sell for a fair price the whole season through.

Hiram was giving his whole heart and soul to the work—he was wrapped up in the effort to make the farm pay. And for good reason.

It was "up to him" to not alone turn a profit for his employer, and himself; but he desired—oh, how strongly!—to show the city folk who had sneered at him that he could be a success in the right environment.

Besides, and in addition, Hiram Strong was ambitious—very ambitious indeed for a youth of his age. He wanted to own a farm of his own in time—and it was no "one-horse farm" he aimed at.

No, indeed! Hiram had read of the scientific farming of the Middle West, and the enormous tracts in the Northwest devoted to grain and other staple crops, where the work was done for the most part by machinery.

He longed to see all this—and to take part in it. He desired the big things in farming, nor would he ever be content to remain a helper.

"I'm going to be my own boss, some day—and I'm going to boss other men. I'll show these fellows around here that I know what I want, and when I get it I'll handle it right!" Hiram soliloquized.

"It's up to me to save every cent I can. Henry thinks I'm niggardly, I expect, because I wouldn't go to town Saturday night with him. But I haven't any money to waste.

"The hundred I'm to get next Christmas from Mrs. Atterson I don't wish to draw on at all. I'll get along with such old clothes as I've got."

Hiram was not naturally a miser; he frequently bought some little thing for Sister when he went to town—a hair-ribbon, or the like, which he knew would please the girl; but for himself he was determined to be saving.

At the end of his contract with Mrs. Atterson he would have two hundred dollars anyway. But that was not the end and aim of Hiram Strong's hopes.

"It's the clause in our agreement about the profits of our second season that is my bright and shining star," he told the good lady more than once. "I don't know yet what we had better put in next year to bring us a fortune; but we'll know before it comes time to plant it."

Meanwhile the wheel-hoe and seeder he had insisted upon Mrs. Atterson buying had arrived, and Hiram, after studying the instructions which came with it, set the machine up as a seed-sower. Later, after the bulk of the seeds were in the ground, he would take off the seeding attachment and bolt on the hoe, or cultivator attachments, with which to stir the soil between the narrower rows of vegetables.

As he made ready to plant seeds such as carrot, parsnip, onion, salsify, and leaf-beet, as well as spring spinach, early turnips, radishes and kohlrabi, Hiram worked that part of his plowed land over again and again with the spike harrow, finally boarding the strips down smoothly as he wished to plant them. The seedbed must be as level as a floor, and compact, for good use to be made of the wheel-seeder.

When he had lined out one row with his garden line, from side to side of the plowed strip, the marking arrangement attached to his seeder would mark the following lines plainly, and at just the distance he desired.

Onions, carrots, and the like, he put in fifteen inches apart, intending to do all the cultivating of those extremely small plants with the wheel-hoe, after they were large enough. But he foresaw the many hours of cultivating before him and marked the rows for the bulk of the vegetables far enough apart, as he had first intended, to make possible the use of the horse-hoe.

Meanwhile he spike-harrowed the potato patch, running cross-wise of the rows to break the crust and keep down the quick-springing weed seeds. The early peas were already above ground and when they were two inches high Hiram ran his 14-tooth cultivator—or "seed harrow" as it is called in some localities—close to the rows so as to throw the soil toward the plants, almost burying them from sight again. This was to give the peas deep rootage, which is a point necessary for the quick and stable growth of this vegetable.

In odd moments Hiram had cut and set a few posts, bought poultry netting in Scoville, and enclosed Mrs. Atterson's chicken-run. She had taken his advice and sent for eggs, and already had four hens setting and expected to set the remainder of the of the eggs in a few days.

Sister took an enormous interest in this poultry-raising venture. She "counted chickens before they were hatched" with a vengeance, and after reading a few of the poultry catalogs she figured out that, in three years, from the increase of Mother Atterson's hundred eggs, the eighty-acre farm would not be large enough to contain the flock.

"And all from five dollars!" gasped Sister. "I don't see why everybody doesn't go to raising chickens—then there'd be no poor folks, everybody would be rich—Well! I expect there'd always have to be institutions for orphans—and boarding houses!"

The new-springing things from the ground, the "hen industry" and the repairing and beautifying of the outside of the farmhouse did not take up all their attention. There were serious matters to be discussed in the evening, after the others had gone to bed, 'twixt Hiram and his employer.

There was the five or six acres of bottom land—the richest piece of soil of the entire eighty. Hiram had not forgotten this, and the second Sunday of their stay at the farm, after the whole family had attended service at a chapel less than half a mile up the road, he had urged Mrs. Atterson to walk with him through the timber to the riverside.

"For the Land o' Goshen!" the ex-boarding house mistress had finally exclaimed. "To think that I own all of this. Why, Hi, it don't seem as if it was so. I can't get used to it. And this timber, you say, is all worth money? And if I cut it off, it will grow up again— —"

"In thirty to forty years the pine will be worth cutting again—and some of the other trees," said Hiram, with a smile.

"Well! that would be something for Sister to look forward to," said the old lady, evidently thinking aloud. "And I don't expect her folks—whoever they be—will ever look her up now, Hiram."

"But with the timber cut and this side hill cleared, you would have a very valuable thirty acres, or so, of tillage—valuable for almost any crop, and early, too, for it slopes toward the sun," said the young farmer, ignoring the other's observation.

"Well, well! it's wonderful," returned Mrs. Atterson.

But she listened attentively to what he had to say about clearing the bottom land, which was a much more easily accomplished task, as Hiram showed her. It would cost something to put the land into shape for late corn, and so prepare it for some more valuable crop the following season.

"Well, nothing ventured, nothing have!" Mrs. Atterson finally agreed. "Go ahead—if it won't cost much more than what you say to get the corn in. I understand it's a gamble, and I'm taking a gambler's chance. If the river rises and floods the corn in June, or July, then we get nothing this season?"

"That is a possibility," admitted Hiram.

"Go ahead," exclaimed Mother Atterson. "I never did know that there was sporting blood in me; but I kinder feel it risin', Hi, with the sap in the trees. We'll chance it!"

Occasionally Hiram had stepped down to the pasture and squinted across to the water-hole. The grass was not long enough yet to turn the cow into the field, so he was obliged to make these special trips to the pasture.

He had seen nothing of the Dickersons—to speak to, that is—since his trouble with Pete. And, of a sudden, just before dinner one noon, Hiram took a look at the pasture and beheld a figure seemingly working down in the corner.

Hiram ran swiftly in that direction. Half-way there he saw that it was Pete, and that he had deliberately cut out a panel of the fence and was letting a pair of horses he had been plowing with, drink at the pool, before he took them home to the Dickerson stable.

Hiram stopped running and recovered his breath before he reached the lower corner of the pasture. Pete saw him coming, and grinned impudently at him.

"What are you doing here, Dickerson?" demanded the young farmer, indignantly.

"Well, if you wanter keep us out, you'd better keep up your fences better," returned Pete. "I seen the wires down, and it's handy——"

"You cut those wires!" interrupted Hiram, angrily.

"You're another," drawled Pete, but grinning in a way to exasperate the young farmer.

"I know you did so."

"Wal, if you know so much, what are you going to do about it?" demanded the other. "I guess you'll find that these wires will snap 'bout as fast as you can mend 'em. Now, you can put that in your pipe an' smoke it!"

"But I don't smoke." Hiram observed, growing calm immediately. There was no use in giving this lout the advantage of showing anger with him.

"Mr. Smartie!" snarled Pete Dickerson. "Now, you see, there's somebody just as smart as you be. These horses have drunk there, and they're going to drink again."

"Is that your father yonder?" demanded Hiram, shortly.

"Yes, it is."

"Call him over here."

"Why, if he comes over here, he'll eat you alive!" cried Pete, laughing. "You don't know my dad."

"I don't; but I want to," Hiram said, calmly. "That's why you'd better call him over. I have got pretty well acquainted with you, and the rest of your family can't be any worse, as I look at it. Call him over," and the young farmer stepped nearer to the lout.

"You call him yourself!" cried Pete, beginning to back away, for he remembered how he had been treated at his previous encounter with Hiram.

Hiram seized the bridles of the work horses, and shook them out of Pete's clutch.

"Tell your father to come here," commanded the young farmer, fire in his eyes. "We'll settle this thing here and now.

"These horses are on Mrs. Atterson's land. I know the county stock law as well as you do. You cut this fence, and your cattle are on her ground.

"It will cost you a dollar a head to get them off again—if Mrs. Atterson wishes to demand it. Now, call your father."

Pete raised a yell which startled the long-legged man striding over the hill toward the Dickerson farmhouse. Hiram saw the older Dickerson turn, stare, and then start toward them.

Pete continued to beckon, and began to yell:

"Dad! Dad! He won't let me have the hosses!"

Sam Dickerson came striding down to the waterhole—a lean, long, sour-looking man he was, with a brown face knotted into a continual scowl, and hard, bony hands. Yet Hiram was not afraid of him.

"What's the trouble here?" growled the farmer.

"He's got the hosses. I told you the fence was down and I was goin' to water 'em——"

"Shut up!" commanded his father, eyeing Hiram. "I'm talking to this fellow: What's the trouble here?"

"Your horses are on Mrs. Atterson's land," Hiram said, quietly. "You know that stock which strays can be held for a dollar a head—damage or no damage to crops. I warn you, keep your horses on your own land."

"That's your fence; if you don't keep it up, who's fault is it if my horses get on your land?" growled Dickerson, evidently making the matter a personal one with Hiram.

"Your boy here cut the wires."

"No I didn't, Dad!" interposed Pete.

Quick as a flash Hiram dropped the bridle reins, sprang for Pete, seized him in a wrestler's grip, twisted him around, and tore from his pocket a pair of heavy wire-cutters.

"What were you doing with these in your pocket, then?" demanded Hiram, disdainfully, tossing the plyers upon the ground at Pete's feet, and stepping back to keep the restless horses from leaving the edge of the water-hole.

Sam Dickerson seemed to take a grim pleasure in his son's overthrow. He growled:

"He's got you there, Pete. You'd better stop monkeyin' around here. Pick up them bridles and come on."

He turned to depart without another word to Hiram; but the latter did not propose to be put off that way.

"Hold on!" he called. "Who's going to mend this fence, Mr. Dickerson?"

Dickerson turned and eyed him coldly again.

"What's that to me? Mend your own fence," he said.

"Then I shall take these horses up to our barn. You can come and settle the matter with Mrs. Atterson—unless you wish to pay me two dollars here and now," said the young farmer, his voice carrying clearly to where the man stood upon the rising ground above him.

"Why, you young whelp!" roared Dickerson, suddenly starting down the slope.

But Hiram Strong neither moved nor showed fear. Somehow, this sturdy young fellow, in the high laced boots, with his flannel shirt open at the throat, raw as was the day, his sleeves rolled back to his elbows, was a figure to make even a more muscular man than Sam Dickerson hesitate.

"Pete!" exclaimed the farmer, harshly, still eyeing Hiram. "Run up to the house and bring my shotgun. Be quick about it."

Hiram said never a word, and the horses, yoked together, began to crop the short grass springing upon the bank of the water-hole.

"You'll find out you're fooling with the wrong man, you whippersnapper!" promised Dickerson.

"You can pay me two dollars and I'll mend the fence; or you can mend the fence and we'll call it square," said Hiram, slowly, and evenly. "I'm a boy, but I'm not to be frightened with a threat— —"

Pete's long legs brought him flying back across the fields. Nothing he had done in a long while pleased him quite as much as this errand.

Hiram turned, jerked at the horses' bridle-reins, turned them around, and with a sharp slap on the nigh one's flank, sent them both trotting up into the Atterson pasture.

"Stop that, you rascal!" cried Dickerson, grabbing the gun from his hopeful son, and losing his head now entirely. "Bring that team back!"

"You mend the fence, and I will," declared Hiram, unshaken.

The angry man sprang down to his level, flourishing the gun in a way that would have been dangerous indeed had Hiram believed it to be loaded. And as it was, the young farmer was very angry.

The right was on his side; if he allowed these Dickersons, father and son, to browbeat him this once, it would only lead to future trouble.

This thing had to be settled right here and now. It would never do for Hiram to show fear. And if both of the long-legged Dickersons pitched upon him, of course, he would be no match for them.

But Sam Dickerson stumbled and almost fell as he reached the edge of the water-hole, and before he could recover himself, Hiram leaped upon him, seized the shotgun, and wrenched it from his hands.

He reversed the weapon in a flash, clubbed it, and raised it over his head with a threatening swing that made Pete yell from the top of the bank:

"Look out, Dad! He's a-goin' ter swat yer!"

Sam tried to scramble out of the way. But down came the gun butt with all the force of Hiram's good muscle, and—the stock was splintered and the lock shattered upon the big stone that here cropped out of the bank.

"There's your gun—what's left of it," panted the young farmer, tossing the broken weapon from him. "Now, don't you ever threaten me with a gun again, for if you do I'll have you arrested.

"We've got to be neighbors, and we've got to get along in a neighborly manner. But I'm not going to allow you to take advantage of Mrs. Atterson, because she is a woman.

"Now, Mr. Dickerson," he added, as the man scrambled up, glaring at him evidently with more surprise than anger, "if you'll make Pete mend this fence, you can have your horses. Otherwise I'm going to 'pound' them according to the stock law of the county."

"Pete," said his father, briefly, "go get your hammer and staples and mend this fence up as good as you found it."

"And now," said Hiram, "I'm going home to gear the horse to the wagon, and I'll drive over to your house, Mr. Dickerson. From time to time you have borrowed while Uncle Jeptha was alive quite a number of tools. I want them. I have made inquiries and I know what tools they are. Just be prepared to put them into my wagon, will you?"

He turned on his heel without further words and left the Dickersons to catch their horses, and to repair the fence—both of which they did promptly.

Not only that, but when Hiram drove into the Dickerson dooryard an hour later he had no trouble about recovering the tools which the neighbor had borrowed and failed to return.

Pete scowled at him and muttered uncomplimentary remarks; but Sam phlegmatically smoked his pipe and sat watching the young farmer without any comment.

"And so, that much is accomplished," ruminated Hiram, as he drove home. "But I'm not sure whether hostilities are finished, or have just begun."

CHAPTER XV
ONE SATURDAY AFTERNOON

"The old Atterson place" as it was called in the neighborhood, began to take on a brisk appearance these days. Sister, with the help of Old Lem Camp, had long since raked the dooryard clean and burned the rubbish which is bound to gather during the winter.

Years before there had been flower beds in front; but Uncle Jeptha had allowed the grass to overrun them. It was a month too early to think of planting many flowers; but Hiram had bought some seeds, and he showed Sister how to prepare boxes for them in the sunny kitchen windows, along with the other plant boxes; and around the front porch he spaded up a strip, enriched it well, and almost the first seeds put into the ground on the farm were the sweet peas around this porch. Mother Atterson was very fond of these flowers and had always managed to coax some of them to grow even in the boarding-house back yard.

At the side porch she proposed to have morning-glories and moonflowers, while the beds in front would be filled with those old-fashioned flowers which everybody loves.

"But if we can't make our own flower-beds, we can go without them, Hi," said the bustling old lady. "We mustn't take you from your other work to spade beds for us. Every cat's got to catch mice on this place, now I tell ye!"

And Hiram certainly was busy enough these days. The early seeds were all in, however, and he had run the seed-harrow over the potato rows again, lengthwise, to keep the weeds out until the young plants should get a start.

Despite the raw winds and frosts at night, the potatoes had come up well and, with the steadily warming wind and sun, would now begin to grow. Other farmers' potatoes in the vicinity were not yet breaking the ground.

Early on Monday morning Henry Pollock appeared with bush-axe and grubbing hoe, and Hiram shouldered similar tools and they started for the river bottom. It was so far from the house that Mrs. Atterson agreed to send their dinner to them.

"Father says he remembers seeing corn growing on this bottom," said Henry, as they set to work, "so high that the ears were as high up as a tall man. It's splendid corn land—if it don't get flooded out."

"And does the river often over-ran its banks?" queried Hiram, anxiously.

"Pretty frequent. It hasn't yet this year; there wasn't much snow last winter, you see, and the early spring floods weren't very high. But if we have a long wet spell, as we do have sometimes as late as July, you'll see water here."

"That's not very encouraging," said Hiram. "Not for corn prospects, at least."

"Well, corn's our staple crop. You see, if you raise corn enough you're sure of feed for your team. That's the main point."

"But people with bigger farms than they have around here can raise corn cheaper than we can. They use machinery in harvesting it, too. Why not raise a better paying crop, and buy the extra corn you may need?"

"Why," responded Henry, shaking his head, "nobody around here knows much about raising fancy crops. I read about 'em in the farm papers— oh, yes, we take papers—the cheap ones. There is a lot of information in 'em, I guess; but father don't believe much that's printed."

"Doesn't believe much that's printed?" repeated Hiram, curiously.

"Nope. He says it's all lies, made up out of some man's head. You see, we useter take books out of the Sunday School library, and we had story papers, too; and father used to read 'em as much as anybody."

"But one summer we had a summer boarder—a man that wrote things. He had one of these dinky little merchines with him that you play on like a piano, you know— —"

"A typewriter?" suggested Hiram, with a smile.

"Yep. Well, he wrote stories. Father learnt as how all that stuff was just imaginary, and so he don't take no stock in printed stuff any more."

"That man just sat down at that merchine, and rattled off a story that he got real money for. It didn't have to be true at all.

"So father soured on it. And he says the stuff in the farm papers is just the same."

"I'm afraid that your father is mistaken there," said Hiram, hiding his amusement. "Men who have spent years in studying agricultural conditions, and experimenting with soils, and seeds, and plants, and fertilizers, and all that, write what facts they have learned for our betterment.

"No trade in the world is so encouraged and aided by Governments, and by private corporations, as the trade of farming. There is scarcely a State which does not have a special agricultural college in which there are winter courses for people who cannot give the open time of the year to practical experiment on the college grounds.

"That is what you need in this locality, I guess," added Hiram. "Some scientific farming."

"Book farming, father calls it," said Henry. "And he says it's no good."

"Why don't you save your money and take a course next winter in some side line and so be able to show him that he's wrong?" suggested Hiram. "I want to do that myself after I have fulfilled my contract with Mrs. Atterson.

"I won't be able to do so next winter, for I shall be on wages. You're going to be a farmer, aren't you?"

"I expect to. We've got a good farm as farms go around here. But it seems about all we can do to pay our fertilizer bills and get a living off it."

"Then why don't you go about fitting yourself for your job?" "asked Hiram. Be a good farmer—an up-to-date farmer.

"No fellow expects to be a machinist, or an electrician, or the like, without spending some time under good instructors. Most that I know about soils, and fertilizers, and plant development, and the like, I learned from my father, who kept abreast of the times by reading and experiment.

"You can stumble along, working at your trade of farming, and only half knowing it all your life; that's what most farmers do, in fact. They are too lazy to take up the scientific side of it and learn why.

"That's the point—learn why you do things that your father did, and his father did, and his father before him. There's usually good reason why they did it—a scientific reason which somebody dug out by experiment ages ago; but you ought to be able to tell why."

"I suppose that's so," admitted Henry, as they worked on, side by side. "But I don't know what father would say if I sprung a college course on him!"

"I'd find out," returned Hiram, laughing. "You'd better spend your money that way than for a horse and buggy. That's the highest ambition of most boys in the country."

The labor of bushing and grubbing these acres of lowland was no light one. Hiram insisted that every stub and root be removed that a heavy plow could not tear out. They had made some progress by noon, however, when Sister came down with their dinner.

Hiram built a campfire over which the coffee was re-heated, and the three ate together, Sister enjoying the picnic to the full. She insisted on helping in the work by piling the brush and roots into heaps for burning, and she remained until midafternoon.

"I like that Henry boy," she confided to Hiram. "He don't pull my braids, or poke fun at me."

But Sister was developing and growing fast these days. She was putting on flesh and color showed in her cheeks. They were no longer hollow and sallow, and she ran like a colt-and was almost as wild.

The work of clearing the bottom land could not be continued daily; but the boys got in three full days that week, and Saturday morning. Henry, did not wish to work on Saturday afternoon, for in this locality almost all the farmers knocked off work at noon Saturday and went to town.

But when Henry shouldered his tools to go home at noon, Sister appeared as usual with the lunch, and she and Hiram cut fishing rods and planned to have a real picnic.

Trout and mullet were jumping in the pools under the bank; and they caught several before stopping to eat their own meal. The freshly caught fish were a fine addition to the repast.

They went back to fishing after a while and caught enough for supper at the farmhouse. Just as they were reeling up their lines the silence of the place was disturbed by a strange sound.

"There's a motorcycle coming!" cried Sister, jumping up and looking all around.

There was a bend in the river below this bottom, and another above; so they could not see far in either direction unless they climbed to the high ground. For a minute Hiram could not tell in which direction the sound was coming; but he knew the steady put-put-put must be the exhaust of a motor-boat.

It soon poked its nose around the lower turn. It was a good-sized boat and instantly Hiram recognized at least one person aboard.

Miss Lettie Bronson, in a very pretty boating costume, was in the bow. There were half a dozen other girls with her—well dressed girls, who were evidently her friends from the St. Beris school at Scoville.

"Oh, oh! what a pretty spot!" cried Lettie, on the instant. "We'll go ashore here and have our luncheon, girls."

She did not see Hiram and Sister for a moment; but the latter tugged at Hiram's sleeve.

"I've seen that girl before," she whispered. "She came in the carriage with the man who spoke to you—you remember? She asked me if I had always lived in the country, and how I tore my frock."

"Isn't she pretty?" returned Hiram.

"Awfully. But I'm not sure that I like her yet."

Suddenly Lettie saw Hiram and the girl beside him. She started, flushed a little, and then gave Hiram a cool little nod and turned her gaze from him. Her manner showed that he was not "down in her good books," and the young fellow flushed in turn.

"I don't know as we'd better try to make the bank here, Miss," said the man who was directing the motor-boat. "The current's mighty sharp."

"I want to land here," said Lettie, decidedly. "It's the prettiest spot we've seen—isn't it, girls?"

Her friends agreed. Hiram, casting a quick eye over the ruffled surface of the river, saw that the man was right. How well the stream below was fitted for motor-boating he did not know; but he was pretty sure that there were too many ledges just under the surface here to make it safe for the boat to go farther.

"I intend to land here-right by that big tree!" commanded Lettie Bronson, stamping her foot.

"Well, I dunno," drawled the man; and just then the bow of the boat swung around, was forced heavily down stream by the current, and slam it went against a reef!

The man shot off the engine instantly. The bow of the boat was lodged on the rock, and tip-tilted considerably. The girls screamed, and Lettie herself was almost thrown into the water, for she was standing.

CHAPTER XVII
MR. PEPPER APPEARS

But Hiram noted again that Lettie Bronson did not display terror. While her friends were screaming and crying, she sat perfectly quiet, and for a minute said never a word.

"Can't you back off?" Hi heard her ask the boatman.

"Not without lightening her, Miss. And she may have smashed a plank up there, too. I dunno."

The Western girl turned immediately to Hiram, who had now come to the bank's edge. She smiled at him charmingly, and her eyes danced. She evidently appreciated the fact that the young farmer had her at a disadvantage—and she had meant to snub him.

"I guess you'll have to help me again, Mr. Strong," she said. "What will we do? Can you push out a plank to us, or something?"

"I'm afraid not, Miss Bronson," he returned. "I could cut a pole and reach it to the boat; but you girls couldn't walk ashore on it."

"Oh, dear! have we got to wade?" cried one of Lettie's friends.

"You can't wade. It's too deep between the shore and the boat," Hiram said, calmly.

"Then—then we'll stay here till the tide rises and dr-dr-drowns us!" wailed another of the girls, giving way to sobs.

"Don't be a goose, Myra Carroll!" exclaimed Lettie. "If you waited here for the tide to rise you'd be gray-haired and decrepit. The tide doesn't rise here. But maybe a spring flood would wash you away."

At that the frightened one sobbed harder than ever. She was one of those who ever see the dark side of adventure. There was no hope on her horizon.

"I dunno what you can do for these girls," said the man. "I'd git out and push off the boat, but I don't dare with them aboard."

But Hiram's mind had not been inactive, if he was standing in seeming idleness. Sister tugged at his sleeve again and whispered:

"Have they got to stay there and drown, Hi?"

"I guess not," he returned, slowly. "Let's see: this old sycamore leans right out over them. I can shin up there with the aid of the big grapevine. Then, if I had a rope — —"

"Shall I run and get one?" demanded Sister, listening to him.

"Hullo!" exclaimed Hiram, speaking to the man in the boat.

"Well?" asked the fellow.

"Haven't you got a coil of strong rope aboard?"

"There's the painter," said the man.

"Toss it ashore here," commanded Hiram.

"Oh, Hiram Strong!" cried Lettie. "You don't expect us to walk tightrope, do you?" and she began to giggle.

"No. I want you to unfasten the end of the rope. I want it clear — that's it," said Hiram. "And it's long enough, I can see."

"For what?" asked Sister.

"Wait and you'll see," returned the young farmer, hastily coiling the rope again.

He hung it over his shoulder and then started to climb the big sycamore. He could go up the bole of this leaning tree very quickly, for the huge grapevine gave him a hand-hold all the way.

"Whatever are you going to do?" cried Lettie Bronson, looking up at him, as did the other girls.

"Now," said Hiram, in the first small crotch of the tree, which was almost directly over the stranded launch, "if you girls have any pluck at all, I can get you ashore, one by one."

"What do you mean for us to do, Hiram?" repeated Lettie.

The young farmer quickly fashioned a noose at the end of the line — not a slipnoose, for that would tighten and hurt anybody bearing upon it. This he dropped down to the boat and Lettie caught it.

"Get your head and shoulders through that noose, Miss Bronson," he commanded. "Let it come under your arms. I will lift you out of the boat and swing you back and forth — there's none of you so heavy that I can't do this, and if you wet your feet a little, what's the odds?"

"Oh, dear! I can never do that!" squealed one of the other girls.

"Guess you'll have to do it if you don't want to stay here all night," returned Lettie, promptly. "I see what you want, Hiram," she added, and quickly adjusted the loop.

"Now, when you swing out over the bank, Sister will grab you, and steady you. It will be all right if you have a care. Now!" cried Hiram.

Lettie Bronson showed no fear at all as he drew her up and she swung out of the boat over the swiftly-running current. Hiram laid along the tree-trunk in an easy position, and began swinging the girl at the end of the rope, like a pendulum.

The river bank being at least three feet higher than the surface of the water; he did not have to shift the rope again as he swung the girl back and forth.

Sister, clinging with her left hand to the grapevine, leaned forward and clutched Lettie's hand. When she seized it, Sister backed away, and the swinging girl landed upright upon the bank.

"Oh, that's fun!" Lettie cried, laughing, loosing herself from "the loop. Now you come, Mary Judson!"

Thus encouraged they responded one by one, and even the girl who had broken down and cried agreed to be rescued by this simple means. The boatman then, after removing his shoes and stockings and rolling up his trousers, stepped out upon the sunken rock and pushed off the boat.

But it was leaking badly. He dared not take aboard his passengers again, but turned around and went down stream as fast as he could go so as to beach the boat in a safe place.

"Now how'll we get back to Scoville?" cried one of Lettie's friends. "I can never walk that far."

Sister had dropped back, shyly, behind Hiram, when he descended the tree. She had aided each girl ashore; but only Lettie had thanked her. Now she tugged at Hiram's sleeve.

"Take 'em home in our wagon," she whispered.

"I can take you to Scoville—or to Miss Bronson's—in the farm wagon," Hiram said, smiling. "You can sit on straw in the bottom and be comfortable."

"Oh, a straw ride!" cried Lettie. "What fun! And he can drive us right to St. Beris—And think what the other girls will say and how they'll stare!"

The idea seemed a happy one to all the girls save the cry-baby, Myra Carroll. And her complaints were drowned in the laughter and chatter of the others.

Hiram picked up the tools, Sister got the string of fish, and they set out for the Atterson farmhouse. Lettie chatted most of the way with Hiram; but to Sister, walking on the other side of the young farmer, the Western girl never said a word.

At the house it was the same. While Hiram was cleaning the wagon and putting a bed of straw into it, and currying the horse and gearing him to the wagon, Mrs. Atterson brought a crock of cookies out upon the porch and talked with the girls from St. Beris. Sister had run indoors and changed her shabby and soiled frock for a new gingham; but when she came down to the porch, and stood bashfully in the doorway, none of the girls from town spoke to her.

Hiram drove up with the farm-wagon. Most of the girls had accepted the adventure in the true spirit now, and they climbed into the wagon-bed on the clean straw with laughter and jokes. But nobody invited Sister to join the party.

The orphan looked wistfully after the wagon as Hiram drove out of the yard. Then she turned, with trembling lip, to Mother Atterson: "She—she's awfully pretty," she said, "and Hiram likes her. But she—they're all proud, and I guess they don't think much of folks like us, after all."

"Shucks, Sister! we're just good as they be, every bit," returned Mrs. Atterson, bruskly.

"I know; mebbe we be," admitted Sister, slowly. "But it don't feel so."

And perhaps Hiram had some such thought, too, after he had driven the girls to the big boarding school in Scoville. For they all got out without even thanking him or bidding him good-bye—all save Lettie.

"Really, we are a thousand times obliged to you, Hiram Strong," she said, in her very best manner, and offering him her hand. "As the girls were my guests I felt I must get them home again safely—and you were indeed a friend in need."

But then she spoiled it utterly, by adding:

"Now, how much do I owe you, Hiram?" and took out her purse. "Is two dollars enough?" This put Hiram right in his place. He saw plainly that, friendly as the Bronsons were, they did not look upon a common farm-boy as their equal—not in social matters, at least.

"I could not take anything for doing a neighbor a favor, Miss Bronson," said Hiram, quietly. "Thank you. Good-day."

Hiram drove back home feeling quite as depressed as Sister, perhaps. Finally he said to himself:

"Well, some day I'll show 'em!"

After that he put the matter out of his mind and refused to be troubled by thoughts of Lettie Bronson, or her attitude toward him.

Spring was advancing apace now. Every day saw the development of bud, leaf and plant. Slowly the lowland was cleared and the brush and roots were heaped in great piles, ready for the torch.

Hiram could not depend upon this six acres as their only piece of corn, however. There was the four-acre lot between the barnyard and the pasture in which he proposed to plant the staple crop.

He drew out the remainder of the coarse manure and spread it upon this land, as far as it would go. For enriching the remainder of the corn crop he would have to depend upon a commercial fertilizer. He drew, too, a couple of tons of lime to be used on this corn land, and left it in heaps to slake.

And then, out of the clear sky of their progress, came a bolt as unexpected as could be. They had been less than a month upon the farm. Uncle Jeptha had not been in his grave thirty days, and Hiram was just getting into the work of running the place, with success looming ahead.

He had refused Mr. Bronson's offer of a position and had elected to stick by Mrs. Atterson. He had looked forward to nothing to disturb the contract between them until the time should be fulfilled.

Yet one afternoon, while he was at work in the garden, Sister came out to him all in a flurry.

"Mis' Atterson wants you! Mis' Atterson wants you!" cried the girl. "Oh, Hiram! something dreadful's going to happen. I know, by the way Mis' Atterson looks. And I don' like the looks o' that man that's come to see her."

Hiram unhooked the horse at the end of the row and left Sister to lead him to the stable. He went into the house after knocking the mud off his boots.

There, sitting in the bright kitchen, was the sharp-featured, snaky-looking man with whom Hiram had once talked in town. He knew his name was Pepper, and that he did something in the real estate line, and insurance, and the like.

"Jest listen to what this man says, Hiram," said Mrs. Atterson, grimly.

"My name's Pepper," began the man, eyeing Hiram curiously.

"So I hear," returned the young farmer.

"Before old Mr. Atterson died we got to talking one day when he was in town about his selling."

"Well?" returned Hiram. "You didn't say anything about that when you offered twelve hundred for this place."

"Well," said the man, stubbornly, "that was a good offer."

Hiram turned to Mrs. Atterson. "Do you want to sell for that price?"

"No, I don't, Hi," she said.

"Then that settles it, doesn't it? Mrs. Atterson is the owner, and she knows her own mind."

"I made Uncle Jeptha a better offer," said Mr. Pepper, "and I'll make Mrs. Atterson the same—sixteen hundred dollars. It's a run-down farm, of course— —"

"If Mrs. Atterson doesn't want to sell," interrupted Hiram, but here his employer intervened.

"There's something more, Hi," she said, her face working "strangely. Tell him, you Pepper!"

"Why, the old man gave me an option on the place, and I risked a twenty dollar bill on it. The option had—er—a year to run; dated February tenth last; and I've decided to take the option up," said Mr. Pepper, his shrewd little eyes dancing in their gaze from Hiram to the old lady and back again.

CHAPTER XVIII
A HEAVY CLOUD

Now, a rattlesnake is poisonous, but he gives fair warning; a swamp moccasin lies in wait for the unwary and strikes without sign or sound. Into Hiram Strong's troubled mind came the thought that Mr. Pepper was striking like his prototype of the swamps.

A snaky sort of a man was Mr. Pepper—sly, a hand-rubber as he talked, with a little, sickly grin playing about his thin, mean mouth. When he opened it Hiram almost expected to see a forked tongue run out.

At least, of one thing was the young farmer sure: Mr. Pepper was no more to be trusted than a serpent. Therefore, he did not take a word that the man said on trust.

He recovered from the shock which the statement of the real estate man had caused, and he uttered no expression of either surprise, or trouble. Mrs. Atterson he could see was vastly disturbed by the statement; but somebody had to keep a cool bead in this matter.

"Let's see your option," Hiram demanded, bruskly.

"Why—if Mrs. Atterson wishes to see it——"

"You show it to Hi, you Pepper-man," snapped the old lady. "I wouldn't do a thing without his advice."

"Oh, well, if you consider a boy's advice material——"

"I know Hi's honest," declared the old lady, tartly. "And that's what I'm sure you ain't! Besides," she added, sadly, "Hi's as much interested in this thing as I be. If the farm's got to be sold, it puts Hi out of a job."

"Oh, very well," said the real estate man, and he drew a rather soiled, folded paper from his inner pocket.

He seemed to hesitate the fraction of a second about showing the paper. It increased Hi's suspicion—this hesitancy. If the man had a perfectly good option on the farm, why didn't he go about the matter boldly?

But when he got the paper in his own hands he could see nothing wrong with it. It seemed written in straight-forward language, the signatures were clear enough, and as he had seen and read Uncle Jeptha's will, he was quite sure that this was the old man's signature to the option which, for the sum of twenty dollars in hand paid to him, he agreed to sell his farm, situated so-and-so, for sixteen hundred dollars, cash, same to be paid over within one year of date.

"Of course," said Hiram, slowly, handing back the paper—indeed, Pepper had kept the grip of his forefinger and thumb on it all the time—"Of course, Mrs. Atterson's lawyer must see this before she agrees to anything."

"Why, Hiram! I ain't got no lawyer," exclaimed the old lady.

"Go to Mr. Strickland, who made Uncle Jeptha's will," Hiram said to her. Then he turned to Pepper:

"What's the name of the witness to that old man's signature?"

"Abel Pollock."

"Oh! Henry's father?"

"Yes. He's got a son named Henry."

"And who's the Notary Public?"

"Caleb Schell. He keeps the store just at the crossroads as you go into town."

"I remember the store," said Hiram, thoughtfully.

"But Hiram!" cried Mrs. Atterson, "I don't want to sell the farm."

"We'll be sure this paper is all straight before you do sell, Mrs. Atterson."

"Why, I just won't sell!" she exclaimed. "Uncle Jeptha never said nothing in his will about giving this option. And that lawyer says that in a couple of years the farm will be worth a good deal more than this Pepper offers."

"Why, Mrs. Atterson!" exclaimed the real estate man, cheerfully, "as property is selling in this locality now, sixteen hundred dollars is a mighty good offer for your farm. You ask anybody. Why, Uncle Jeptha knew it was; otherwise he wouldn't have given me the option, for he didn't believe I'd come up with the price. He knew it was a high offer."

"And if it's worth so much to you, why isn't it worth more to Mrs. Atterson to keep?" demanded Hiram, sharply.

"Ah! that's my secret—why I want it," said Pepper, nodding. "Leave that to me. If I get bit by buying it, I shall have to suffer for my lack of wisdom."

"You ain't bought it yet—you Pepper," snapped Mrs. Atterson.

"But I'm going to buy it, ma'am," replied he, rather viciously, as he stood up, ready to depart. "I shall expect to hear from you no later than Monday."

"I won't sell it!"

"You'll have to. If you refuse to sign I'll go to the Chancery Court. I'll make you."

"Well. Mebbe you will. But I don't know. I never was made to do anything yet. By no man named Pepper—you can take that home with you," she flung after him as he walked out and climbed into the buggy.

But whereas Mrs. Atterson showed anger, Hiram went back to work in the field with a much deeper feeling racking his mind. If the option was all right—and of course it must be—this would settle their occupancy of the farm.

Of course he could not hold Mrs. Atterson to her contract. She could not help the situation that had now arisen.

His Spring's work had gone for nothing. Sixteen hundred dollars, even in cash, would not be any great sum for the old lady. And she had burdened herself with the support of Sister—and with Old Lem Camp, too!

"Surely, I can't be a burden on her. I'll have to hustle around and find another job. I wonder if Mr. Bronson would take me on now?"

But he knew that the Westerner already had a man who suited him, since Hiram had refused the chance Bronson offered. And, then, Lettie had shown that she felt he had not appreciated their offer. Perhaps her father felt the same way.

Besides, Hiram had a secret wish not to put himself under obligation to the Bronsons. This feeling may have sprung from a foolish source; nevertheless it was strong with the young farmer.

It looked very much to him as though this sudden turn of circumstances was "a facer". If Mrs. Atterson had to sell the farm he was likely to be thrown on his own resources again.

For his own selfish sake Hiram was worried, too. After all, he would be unable to "make good" and to show people that he could make the old, run-down farm pay a profit to its owner.

But Hiram Strong couldn't believe it.

The more he milled over the thing in his mind, the less he understood why Uncle Jeptha, who was of acute mind right up to the hour of his death, so all the neighbors said, should have neglected to speak about the option he had given Pepper on the farm.

And here they were, right in the middle of the Spring work, with crops in the ground and—as Mrs. Atterson agreed—it would be too late to go hunting a farm for this present season.

But Hiram kept to work. He had Sister and Old Lem Camp out in the garden, hand-weeding and thinning the carrots, onions, and other tender plants. That Saturday he went through the entire garden—that part already planted—with either the horse cultivator, or his wheel-hoe.

In planting parsnips, carrots, and other slow-germinating seeds, he had mixed a few radish seed in the seeding machine; these sprang up quickly and defined the rows, so that the space between rows could be cultivated before the other plants had scarcely broke the surface of the soil.

Now these radish were beginning to be big enough to pull. Hiram brought in a few bunches for their dinner on Saturday—the first fruits of the garden.

"Now, I dunno why it is," said Mrs. Atterson, complacently, after setting her teeth in the first radish and relishing its crispness, "but this seems a whole lot better than the radishes we used to buy in Crawberry. I 'spect what's your very own always seems better than other folks's," and she sighed and shook her head.

She was thinking of the thing she had to face on Monday. Hiram hated to see them all so downhearted. Sister's eyes were red from weeping; Old Lem Camp sat at the table, muttering and playing with his food again instead of eating.

But Hiram felt as though he could not give up to the disaster that had come to them. The thought that—in some way—Pepper was taking an unfair advantage of Mother Atterson knocked continually at the door of his mind.

He went over, to himself, all that had passed in the kitchen the day before when the real estate man had come to speak with Mrs. Atterson. How had Pepper spoken about the option? Hadn't there been some hesitancy in the fellow's manner—in his speech, indeed? Just what had Pepper said? Hiram concentrated his mind upon this one thing. What had the man said?

"The option had—er—one year to run."

Those were the fellow's very words. He hesitated before he pronounced the length of time. And he was not a man who, in speaking, had any stammering of tongue.

Why had he hesitated? Why should it trouble him to state the time limit of the option?

Was it because he was speaking a falsehood?

The thought stung Hiram like a thorn in the flesh. He put away the tool with which he was working, slipped on a coat, and started for Henry Pollock's house, which lay not more than half a mile from the Atterson farm, across the fields.

CHAPTER XIX
THE REASON WHY

HIRAM found Abel Pollock mending harness in the shed. Hiram opened his business bluntly, and told the farmer what was up. Mr. Pollock scratched his head, listened attentively, and then sat down to digest the news.

"You gotter move—jest when you've got rightly settled on that place?" he demanded. "Well, that's 'tarnal bad! And from what Henry tells me, you're a young feller with idees, too."

"I don't care so much for myself," Hiram hastened to say. "It's Mrs. Atterson I'm thinking about. And she had just made up her mind that she was anchored for the rest of her life. Besides, I don't think it is a wise thing to sell the property at that price."

"No. I wouldn't sell if I was her, for no sixteen hundred dollars."

"But she's got to, you see, Mr. Pollock. Pepper has the option signed by her Uncle Jeptha——"

"Jeptha Atterson was no fool," interrupted Pollock. "I can't understand his giving an option on the farm, with all this talk of the railroad crossing the river."

"But, Mr. Pollock!" exclaimed Hiram, eagerly, "you must know all about this option. You signed as a witness to Uncle Jeptha's signature."

"No! you don't mean that?" exclaimed the farmer. "My name to it, too?"

"Yes. And it was signed before Caleb Schell the notary public."

"So it was—so it was, boy!" declared the other, suddenly smiting his knee. "I remember I witnessed Uncle Jeptha's signature once. But that was way back there in the winter—before he was took sick."

"Yes, sir?" said Hiram, eagerly.

"That was an option on the old farm. So it was. But goodness me, boy, Pepper must have got him to renew it, or something. That option wouldn't have run till now."

Hiram told him the date the paper was executed.

"That's right, by Jo! It was in February."

"And it was for a year?"

Mr. Pollock stared at him in silence, evidently thinking deeply.

"If you remember all about it, then," Hiram continued, "it's hardly worth while going to Mr. Schell, I suppose."

"I remember, all right," said Pollock, slowly. "It was all done right there in Cale Schell's store. It was one rainy afternoon. There was several of us sitting around Cale's stove. Pepper was one of us. In comes Uncle Jeptha. Pepper got after him right away, but sort of on the quiet, to one side.

"I heard 'em. Pepper had made him an offer for the farm that was 'way down low, and the old man laughed at him.

"We hadn't none of us heard then the talk that came later about the railroad. But Pepper has a brother-in-law who's in the office of the company, and he thinks he gits inside information.

"So, for some reason, he thought the railroad was going to touch Uncle Jeptha's farm. O' course, it ain't. It's goin' over the river by Ayertown.

"I don't see what Pepper wants to take up the option for, anyway. Unless he sees that you're likely to make suthin' out o' the old place, and mebbe he's got a city feller on the string, to buy it."

"It doesn't matter what his reason is. Mrs. Atterson doesn't want to sell, and if that option is all right, she must," said Hiram. "And you are sure Uncle Jeptha gave it for twelve months?"

"Twelve months?" ejaculated Pollock, suddenly. "Why—no—that don't seem right," stammered the farmer, scratching his head.

"But that's the way the option reads."

"Well—mebbe. I didn't just read it myself—no, sir. They jest says to me:

"'Come here, Pollock, and witness these signatures' So, I done it—that's all. But I see Cale put on his specs and read the durn thing through before he stamped it. Yes, sir. Cale's the carefulest notary public we ever had around here.

"Say!" said Mr. Pollock. "You go to Cale and ask him. It don't seem to me the old man give Pepper so long a time."

"For how long was the option to run, then?" queried Hiram, excitedly.

"Wal, I wouldn't wanter say. I don't wanter git inter trouble with no neighbor. If Cale says a year is all right, then I'll say so, too. I wouldn't jest trust my memory."

"But there is some doubt in your mind, Mr. Pollock?"

"There is. A good deal of doubt," the farmer assured him. "But you ask Cale."

This was all that Hiram could get out of the elder Pollock. It was not very comforting. The young farmer was of two minds whether he should see Caleb Schell, or not.

But when he got back to the house for supper, and saw the doleful faces of the three waiting there, he couldn't stand inaction.

"If you don't mind, I want to go to town tonight, Mrs. Atterson," he told the old lady.

"All right, Hiram. I expect you've got to look out for yourself, boy. If you can get another job, you take it. It's a 'tarnal shame you didn't take up with that Bronson's offer when he come here after you."

"You needn't feel so," said Hiram. "You're no more at fault than I am. This thing just happened — nobody could foretell it. And I'm just as sorry as I can be for you, Mother Atterson."

The old woman wiped her eyes.

"Well, Hi, there's other things in this world to worry over besides gravy, I find," she said. "Some folks is born for trouble, and mebbe we're some of that kind."

It was not exactly Mr. Pollock's doubts that sent Hiram Strong down to the crossroads store that evening. For the farmer had seemed so uncertain that the boy couldn't trust to his memory at all.

No. It was Hiram's remembrance of Pepper's stammering when he spoke about the option. He hesitated to pronounce the length of time the option had been drawn for. Was it because he knew there was some trick about the time-limit?

Had the real estate man fooled old Uncle Jeptha in the beginning? The dead man had been very shrewd and careful. Everybody said so.

He was conscious and of acute mind right up to his death. If there was an option on the farm be surely would have said something about it to Mr. Strickland, or to some of the neighbors.

It looked to Hiram as though the old farmer must have believed that the option had expired before the day of his death.

Had Pepper only got the old man's promise for a shorter length of time, but substituted the paper reading "one year" when it was signed? Was that the mystery?

However, Hiram could not see how that would help Mrs. Atterson, for even testimony of witnesses who heard the discussion between the dead man and the real estate agent, could not controvert a written instrument. The young fellow knew that.

He harnessed the old horse to the light wagon and drove to the crossroads store kept by Caleb Schell. Many of the country people liked to trade with this man because his store was a social gathering-place.

Around a hot stove in the winter, and a cold stove at this time of year, the men gathered to discuss the state of the country, local politics, their neighbors' business, and any other topic which was suggested to their more or less idle minds.

On the outskirts of the group of older loafers, the growing crop of men who would later take their places in the soap-box forum lingered; while sky-larking about the verge of the crowd were smaller boys who were learning no good, to say the least, in attaching themselves to the older members of the company.

There will always be certain men in every community who take delight in poisoning the minds of the younger generation. We muzzle dogs, or shoot them when they go mad. The foul-mouthed man is far more vicious than the dog, and should be impounded.

Hiram hitched his horse to the rack before the store and entered the crowded place. The fumes of tobacco smoke, vinegar, cheese, and various other commodities gave a distinctive flavor to Caleb Schell's store—and not a pleasant one, to Hiram's mind.

Ordinarily he would have made any purchases he had to make, and gone out at once. But Schell was busy with several customers at the counter and he was forced to wait a chance to speak with the old man.

One of the first persons Hiram saw in the store was young Pete Dickerson, hanging about the edge of the crowd. Pete scowled at him and moved away. One of the men holding down a cracker-keg sighted Hiram and hailed him in a jovial tone:

"Hi, there, Mr. Strong! What's this we been hearin' about you? They say you had a run-in with Sam Dickerson. We been tryin' to git the pertic'lars out o' Pete, here, but he don't seem ter wanter talk about it," and the man guffawed heartily.

"Hear ye made Sam give back the tools he borrowed of the old man?" said another man, whom Hiram knew to be Mrs. Larriper's son-in-law.

"You are probably misinformed," said Hiram, quietly. "I know no reason why Mr. Dickerson and I should have trouble—unless other neighbors make trouble for us."

"Right, boy—right!" called Cale Schell, from behind the counter, where he could hear and comment upon all that went on in the middle of the room, despite the attention he had to give to his customers.

"Well, if you can git along with Sam and Pete, you'll do well," laughed another of the group.

The Dickersons seemed to be in disfavor in the community, and nobody cared whether Pete repeated what was said to his father, or not.

"I was told," pursued the first speaker, screwing up one eye and grinning at Hiram, "that you broke Sam's gun over his head and chased Pete a mile. That right, son?"

"You will get no information from me," returned Hiram, tartly.

"Why, Pete ought to be big enough to lick you alone, Strong," continued the tantalizer. "Hey, Pete! Don't sneak out. Come and tell us why you didn't give this chap the lickin' you said you was going to?"

Pete only glared at him and slunk out of the store. Hiram turned his back on the whole crowd and waited at the end of the counter for Mr. Schell. The storekeeper was a tall, portly man, with a gray mustache and side-whiskers, and a high bald forehead.

"What can I do for you, Mr. Strong?" he asked, finally having got rid of the customers who preceded Hiram.

Hiram, in a low voice, explained his mission. Schell nodded his head at once.

"Oh, yes," he said; "I remember about the option. I had forgotten it, for a fact; but Pepper was in here yesterday talking about it. He had been to your house."

"Then, sir, to the best of your remembrance, the option is all right?"

"Oh, certainly! Pollock witnessed it, and I put my seal on it. Yes, sir; Pepper can make the old lady sell. It's too bad, if she wants to remain there; but the price he is to pay isn't so bad——"

"You have no reason to doubt the validity of the option?" cried Hiram, in desperation.

"Assuredly not."

"Then why didn't Uncle Jeptha speak of it to somebody before he died, if the option had not run out at that time?"

"Humph!"

"You grant the old man was of sound mind?"

"Sound as a pine knot," agreed the storekeeper, still reflective.

"Then how is it he did not speak to his lawyer about the option when he saw Mr. Strickland within an hour of his death?"

"That does seem peculiar," admitted the storekeeper, slowly.

"And Mr. Pollock says he thinks there is something wrong about the option," went on Hiram, eagerly.

"Oh, Pollock! Pah!" returned Schell. "I don't suppose he even read it."

"But you did?"

"Assuredly. I always read every paper. If they don't want me to know what the agreement is, they can take it to some other Notary," declared the storekeeper with a jolly laugh.

"And you are sure that the option was to run a year?"

"Of course the option's all right—Hold on! A year, did you say? Why—seems to me—let's look this thing up," concluded Caleb Schell, suddenly.

He dived into his little office and produced a ledger from the safe. This he slapped down on the counter between them.

"I'm a careful man, I am," he told Hiram. "And I flatter myself I've got a good memory, too. Pepper was in here yesterday sputtering about the option and I remember now that he spoke of its running a year.

"But it seems to me," said Schell, pawing over the leaves of his ledger, "that the talk between him and old Uncle Jeptha was for a short time. The old man was mighty cautious—mighty cautious."

"That's what Mr. Pollock says," cried Hiram, eagerly.

"But you've seen the option?

"Yes."

"And it reads a year?

"Oh, yes."

"Then how you going to get around that?" demanded Schell, with conviction.

"But perhaps Uncle Jeptha signed the option thinking it was for a shorter time."

"That wouldn't help you none. The paper was signed. And why should Pepper have buncoed him—at that time?"

"Why should he be so eager to get the farm now?" asked Hiram.

"Well, I'll tell you. It ain't out yet. But two or three days ago the railroad board abandoned the route through Ayertown and it is agreed that the new bridge will be built along there by your farm somewhere.

"The river is as narrow there as it is anywhere for miles up and down, and they will stretch a bridge from the high bank on your side, across the meadows, to the high bank on the other side. It will cut out grades, you see. That's what has started Pepper up to grab off the farm while the option is valid."

"But, Mr. Schell, is the option valid?" cried Hiram, anxiously.

"I don't see how you're going to get around it. Ah! here's the place. When I have sealed a paper I make a note of it—what the matter was about and who the contracting parties were. I've done that for years. Let—me—see."

He adjusted his spectacles. He squinted at the page, covered closely with writing. Hiram saw him whispering the words he read to himself. Suddenly the blood flooded into the old man's face, and he looked up with a start at his interrogator.

"Do you mean to say that option's for a year? he demanded.

"That is the way it reads—now," whispered Hiram, watching him closely.

The old man turned the book around slowly on the counter. His stubbed finger pointed to the two or three scrawled lines written in a certain place.

Hiram read them slowly, with beating heart.

CHAPTER XX
AN ENEMY IN THE DARK

The whispered conference between Hiram Strong and the storekeeper could not be heard by the curious crowd around the cold stove; nor did it last for long.

Caleb Schell finally closed his ledger and put it away. Hiram shook hands with him and walked out.

On the platform outside, which was illuminated by a single smoky lantern, a group of small boys were giggling, and they watched Hiram unhitch the old horse and climb into the spring wagon with so much hilarity that the young farmer expected some trick.

The horse started off all right, he missed nothing from the wagon, and so he supposed that he was mistaken. The boys had merely been laughing at him because he was a stranger.

But as Hiram got some few yards from the hitching rack, the seat was suddenly pulled from under him, and he was left sprawling on his back in the bottom of the wagon.

A yell of derision from the crowd outside the store assured him that this was the cause of the boys' hilarity. Luckily his old horse was of quiet disposition, and he stopped dead in his tracks when the seat flew out of the back of the wagon.

A joke is a joke. No use in showing wrath over this foolish amusement of the crossroads boys. But Hiram got a little the best of them, after all.

The youngsters had scattered when the "accident" occurred. Hiram, getting out to pick up the seat, found the end of a strong hemp line fastened to it. The other end was tied to the hitching rack in front of the store.

Instead of casting off the line from the seat, Hiram walked back to the store and cast that end off.

"At any rate, I'm in a good coil of hemp rope," he said to one of the men who had come out to see the fun. "The fellow who owns it can come and prove property; but I shall ask a few questions of him."

There was no more laughter. The young farmer walked back to his wagon, set up the seat again, and drove on.

The roadway was dark, but having been used all his life to country roads at night, Hiram had no difficulty in seeing the path before him. Besides, the old horse knew his way home.

He drove on some eighth of a mile. Suddenly he felt that the wagon was not running true. One of the wheels was yawing. He drew in the old horse; but he was not quick enough.

The nigh forward wheel rolled off the end of the axle, and down came the wagon with a crash!

Hiram was thrown forward and came sprawling—on hands and knees—upon the ground, while the wheel rolled into the ditch. He was little hurt, although the accident might have been serious.

And in truth, he knew it to be no accident. A burr does not easily work off the end of an axle. He had greased the old wagon just before he started for the store, and he knew he had replaced each nut carefully.

This was a deliberately malicious trick—no boy's joke like the tying of the rope to his wagon seat. And the axle was broken. Although he had no lantern he could see that the wagon could not be used again without being repaired.

"Who did it?" was Hiram's unspoken question, as he slowly unharnessed the old horse, and then dragged the broken wagon entirely out of the road so that it would not be an obstruction for other vehicles.

His mind set instantly upon Pete Dickerson. He had not seen the boy when he came out of the crossroads store. If the fellow had removed this burr, he had done it without anybody seeing him, and had then run home.

The young farmer, much disturbed over this incident, mounted the back of the old horse, and paced home. He only told Mrs. Atterson that he had met with an accident and that the light wagon would have to be repaired before it could be used again.

That necessitated their going to town on Monday in the heavy wagon. And Hiram dragged the spring wagon to the blacksmith shop for repairs, on the way.

But before that, the enemy in the dark had struck again. When Hiram went to the barnyard to water the stock, Sunday morning, he found that somebody had been bothering the pump.

The bucket, or pump-valve, was gone. He had to take it apart, cut a new valve out of sole leather, and put the pump together again.

"We'll have to get a cross dog, if we remain here," he told Mrs. Atterson. "There is somebody in the neighborhood who means us harm."

"Them Dickersons!" exclaimed Mrs. Atterson.

"Perhaps. That Pete, maybe. If I once caught him up to his tricks I'd make him sorry enough."

"Tell the constable, Hi," cried Sister, angrily.

"That would make trouble for his folks. Maybe they don't know just how mean Pete is. A good thrashing—and the threat of another every time he did anything mean—would do him lots more good."

This wasn't nice Sunday work, but it was too far to carry water from the house to the horse trough, so Hiram had to repair the pump.

On Monday morning he routed out Sister and Mr. Camp at daybreak. He had been up and out for an hour himself, and on a bench under the shed he had heaped two or three bushels of radishes which he had pulled and washed, ready for bunching.

He showed his helpers how the pretty scarlet balls were to be bunched, and found that Sister took hold of the work with nimble fingers, while Mr. Camp did very well at the unaccustomed task.

"I don't know, Hi," said Mrs. Atterson, despondently, "that it's worth while your trying to sell any of the truck, if we're going to leave here so soon."

"We haven't left yet," he returned, trying to speak cheerfully. "And you might as well get every penny back that you can. Perhaps an arrangement can be made whereby we can stay and harvest the garden crop, at any rate."

"You can make up your mind that that Pepper man won't give us any leeway; he isn't that kind," declared Mother Atterson, with conviction.

Hiram made a quick sale of the radishes at several of the stores, where he got eighteen cents a dozen bunches; but some he sold at the big boarding-school—St. Beris—at a retail price.

"You can bring any other fresh vegetables you may have from time to time," the housekeeper told him. "Nobody ever raised any early vegetables about Scoville before. They are very welcome."

"Once we get a-going," said Hiram to Mrs. Atterson, "you or Sister can drive in with the spring wagon and dispose of the surplus vegetables. And you might get a small canning outfit—they come as cheap as fifteen dollars—and put up tomatoes, corn, peas, beans, and other things. Good canned stuff always sells well."

"Good Land o' Goshen, Hiram!" exclaimed the old lady, in desperation. "You talk jest as though we were going to stay on the farm."

"Well, let's go and see Mr. Strickland," replied the young farmer, and they set out for the lawyer's office.

Mrs. Atterson sat in the ante-room while Hiram asked to speak with the old lawyer in private for a minute. The conference was not for long, and when Hiram came back to his employer he said:

"Mr. Strickland has sent his junior clerk out for Pepper. He thinks we'd better talk the matter over quietly. And he wants to see the option, too."

"Oh, Hiram! There ain't no hope, is there?" groaned the old lady.

"Well, I tell you what!" exclaimed the young fellow, "we won't give in to him until we have to. Of course, if you refuse to sign a deed he can go to chancery and in the end you will have to pay the costs of the action.

"But perhaps, even at that, it might be well to hold him off until you have got the present crop out of the ground."

"Oh, I won't go to law," said Mrs. Atterson, decidedly. "No good ever come of that."

After a time Mr. Strickland invited them both into his private office. The attorney spoke quietly of other matters while they waited for Pepper.

But the real estate man did not appear. By and by Mr. Strickland's clerk came back with the report that Pepper had been called away suddenly on important business.

"They tell me he went Saturday," said the clerk. "He may not be back for a week. But he said he was going to buy the Atterson place when he returned—he's told several people around town so."

"Ah!" said Mr. Strickland, slowly. "Then he has left that threat hanging, like the Sword of Damocles—over Mrs. Atterson's head?"

"I don't know nothin' about that sword, Mr. Strickland, nor no other sword, 'cept a rusty one that my father carried when he was a hoss-sodger in the Rebellion," declared Mother Atterson, nervously. "But if that Pepper man's got one belonging to Mr. Damocles, I shouldn't be at all surprised. That Pepper looked to me like a man that would take anything he could lay his hands on—if he warn't watched!"

"Which is a true and just interpretation of Pepper's character, I believe," observed the lawyer, smiling.

"And we've got to give up the farm at his say-so—at any time?" demanded the old lady.

"If his option is good," said Mr. Strickland. "But I want to see the paper—and I can assure you, Mrs. Atterson, that I shall subject it to the closest possible scrutiny.

"There is a possibility that Pepper's option may be questioned before the courts. Do not build too many hopes on this," he added, quickly, seeing the old lady's face light up.

"You have a very good champion in this young man," and the lawyer nodded at Hiram.

"He suspected all was not right with the option and he has dug up the fact that the witness to your uncle's signature, and the man before whom the paper was attested, both believed the option was for a short time.

"Caleb Schell's book shows that it was for thirty days. Uncle Jeptha undoubtedly thought it was for that length of time and therefore the option expired several days before he died.

"Mr. Pepper may have fallen under temptation. He considered heretofore, like everybody else, that the railroad would pass us by in this section. Pepper gambled twenty dollars on its coming along the boundary of the Atterson farm—between you and Darrell's tract—and thought he had lost.

"Then suddenly the railroad board turned square around and voted for the condemnation of the original route. Pepper remembered the option he had risked twenty dollars on. If it was originally for thirty days, it was void, of course; but Uncle Jeptha is dead, and he hopes perhaps, that nobody else will dispute the validity of it."

"It's a forgery, then?" cried Mrs. Atterson.

"It may be a forgery. We do not know," said the lawyer, hastily. "At any rate, he has the paper, and he is a shrewd rascal."

Mrs. Atterson's face was a study.

"Do you mean to tell me we have got to lose the farm?" she demanded.

"My dear lady, that I cannot tell you. I must see this option. We must put it to the test— —"

"But Schell and Pollock will testify that the option was for thirty days," cried Hiram.

"Perhaps. To the best of their remembrance and belief, it was for thirty days. A shrewd lawyer, however—and Pepper would employ a shrewd one—would turn their evidence inside out.

"No evidence—in theory, at least—can controvert a written instrument, signed, sealed, and delivered. Even Cale Schell's memoranda book cannot be taken as evidence, save in a contributory way. It is not direct. It is the carelessly scribbled record, in pencil, of a busy man.

"No. If Pepper puts forward the option we have got to see if that option has been tampered with—the paper itself, I mean. If the fellow substituted a different instrument, at the time of signing, from the one Uncle Jeptha thought he signed, you have no case—I tell you frankly, my dear lady."

"Then, it ain't no use. We got to lose the place, Hiram," said Mrs. Atterson, when they left the lawyer's office.

"I wouldn't lose heart. If Pepper is scared, he may not trouble you again."

"It's got ten months more to run," said she. "He can keep us guessin' all that time."

"That is so," agreed Hiram, nodding thoughtfully. "But, of course, as Mr. Strickland says, by raising a doubt as to the validity of the option we can hold him off for a while—maybe until we have made this year's crop."

"It's goin' to make me lay awake o' nights," sighed the old lady. "And I thought I'd got through with that when I stopped worryin' about the gravy."

"Well, we won't talk about next year," agreed Hiram. "I'll do the best I can for you through this season, if Pepper will let us alone. We've got the bottom land practically cleared; we might as well plough it and put in the corn there. If we make a crop you'll get all your money back and more. Mr. Strickland told me privately that the option, unless it read that way, would not cover the crops in the ground. And I read the option carefully. Crops were not mentioned."

So it was decided to go ahead with the work as already planned; but neither the young farmer, nor his employer, could look forward cheerfully to the future.

The uncertainty of what Pepper would eventually do was bound to be in their thought, day and night.

CHAPTER XXI
THE WELCOME TEMPEST

To some youths this matter of the option would have been such a clog that they would have lost interest and slighted the work. But not so with Hiram Strong.

He counted this day a lost one, however; he hated to leave the farm for a minute when there was so much to do.

But the next morning he got the plow into the four-acre corn lot; and he did nothing but the chores that week until the ground was entirely plowed. Then Henry Pollock came over and gave him another day's work and they finished grubbing the lowland.

The rubbish was piled in great heaps down there, ready for burning. As long as the rain held off, Hiram did not put fire to the bush-heaps.

But early in the following week the clouds began to gather in a quarter for rain, and late in the afternoon, when the air was still, he took a can of coal oil, and with Sister and Mr. Camp, and even Mrs. Atterson, at his heels, went down to the riverside to burn the brush heaps.

"There's not much danger of the fire spreading to the woods; but if it should," Hiram said, warningly, "it might, at this time of year, do your timber a couple of hundred dollars' worth of damage."

"Goodness me!" exclaimed Mother Atterson. "It does seem ridiculous to hear you talk that a-way. I never owned nothin' but a little bit of furniture before, and I expected the boarders to tear that all to pieces. I'm beginning to feel all puffed up and wealthy."

Hiram cut them all green pineboughs for beaters, and then set the fires, one after another. There were more than twenty of the great piles and soon the river bottom, from bend to bend, was filled with rolling clouds of smoke. As the dusk dropped, the yellow glare of the fire illuminated the scene.

Sister clapped her hands and cried:

"Ain't this bully? It beats the Fourth of July celebration in Crawberry. Oh, I'd rather be on the farm than go to heaven!"

They had brought their supper with them, and leaving the others to watch the fires, and see that the grass did not tempt the flames to the edge of the wood, Hiram cast bait into the river and, in an hour, drew out enough mullet and "bull-heads" to satisfy them all, when they were broiled over the hot coals of the first bonfire to be lighted.

They ate with much enjoyment. Between nine and ten o'clock the fires had all burned down to coals.

A circle of burned-over grass and rubbish surrounded each fire. There seemed no possibility that the flames could spread to the mat of dry leaves on the side hill.

So they went home, a lantern guiding their feet over the rough path through the timber, stopping at the spring for a long, thirst-quenching draught.

The sky was as black as ink. Now and again a faint flash in the westward proclaimed a tempest in that direction. But not a breath of wind was stirring, and the rain might not reach this section.

A dull red glow was reflected on the clouds over the river-bottom. When Hiram looked from his window, just as he was ready for bed, that glow seemed to have increased.

"Strange," he muttered. "It can't be that those fires have spread. There was no chance for them to spread. I—don't—understand it!"

He sat at the window and stared out through the darkness. There was little wind as yet; it was a fact, however, that the firelight flickered on the low-hung clouds with increasing radiance.

"Am I mad?" demanded the young farmer, suddenly leaping up and drawing on his garments again. "That fire is spreading."

He dressed fully, and ran softly down the stairs and left the house. When he came out in the clear the glow had not receded. There was a fire down the hillside, and it seemed increasing every moment.

He remembered the enemy in the dark, and without stopping to rouse the household, ran on toward the woods, his heart beating heavily in his bosom.

Slipping, falling at times, panting heavily because of the rough ground, Hiram came at last through the more open timber to the brink of that steep descent, at the bottom of which lay the smoky river-bottom.

And indeed, the whole of the lowland seemed filled with stifling clouds of smoke. Yet, from a dozen places along the foot of the hill, yellow flames were starting up, kindling higher, and devouring as fast as might be the leaves and tinder left from the wrack of winter.

The nearest bonfire had been a hundred yards from the foot of this hill. His care, Hiram knew, had left no chance of the dull coals in any of the twenty heaps spreading to the verge of the grove.

Man's hand had done this. An enemy, waiting and watching until they had left the field, had stolen down, gathered burning brands, and spread them along the bottom of the hill, where the increasing wind might scatter the fire until the whole grove was in a blaze.

Not only was Mrs. Atterson's timber in danger, but Darrell's tract and that lying beyond would be overwhelmed by the flames if they were allowed to spread.

On the other side, Dickerson had cut his timber a year or two before, clear to the river. The fire would not burn far over his line. Whoever had done this dastardly act, Dickerson's property would not be damaged.

But Hiram lent no time to trouble. His work was cut out for him right here and now—and well he knew it!

He had brought the small axe with him, having caught it up from the doorstep. Now he used it to cut a green bough, and then ran with the latter down the hill and set upon the fire-line like a madman.

The smoke, spread here and there by puffs of rising wind, half choked him. It stung his eyes until they distilled water enough to blind him. He thrashed and fought in the fumes and the murk of it, stumbling and slipping, one moment half-knee deep in quick-springing flames, the next almost overpowered by the smudge that rose from the beaten mat of leaves and rubbish.

It was a lone fight. He had to do it all. There had been no time to rouse either the neighbors, or the rest of the family.

If he did not overcome these flames—and well he knew it—Mother Atterson would arise in the morning to see all her goodly timber scorched, perhaps ruined!

"I must beat it out—beat it out!" thought Hiram, and the repetition of the words thrummed an accompaniment upon the drums of his ears as he thrashed away with a madman's strength.

For no sane person would have tackled such a hopeless task. Before him the flames suddenly leaped six feet or more into the air. They overtopped him as they writhed through a clump of green-briars. The wind puffed the flame toward him, and his face was scorched by the heat.

He lost his eyebrows completely, and the hair was crisped along the front brim of his hat.

Then with a laughing crackle, as though scorning his weakness, the flames ran up a climbing vine and the next moment wrapped a tall pine in lurid yellow.

This pine, like a huge torch, began to give off a thick, black smoke. Would some wakeful neighboring farmer, seeing it, know the danger that menaced and come to Hiram's help?

For yards he had beaten flat the flames and stamped out every spark. Behind him was naught but rolling smoke. It was dark there. No flames were eating up the slope.

But toward Darrell's tract the fire seemed on the increase. He could not catch up with it. And this solitary, sentinel pine, ablaze now in all its head, threatened to fling sparks for a hundred yards.

If the wind continued to rise, the forest was doomed!

His green branch had burned to a crisp. He had lost his axe in the darkness and the smoke, and now he tore another bough, by main strength, from its parent stem.

Hiram Strong worked as though inspired; but to no purpose in the end. For the flames increased. Puff after puff of wind drove the fire on, scattering brands from the blazing pine; and now another, and another, tree caught. The glare of the conflagration increased.

He flung down the useless bough. Fire was all about him. He had to leap suddenly to one side to escape a burst of flame that had caught in a jungle of green-briars.

Then, of a sudden, a crash of thunder rolled and reverberated through the glen. Lightning for an instant lit up the meadows and the river. The glare of it almost blinded the young farmer and, out of the line of fire, he sank to the earth and covered his eyes, seared by the sudden, compelling light.

Again and again the thunder rolled, following the javelins of lightning that seemed to dart from the clouds to the earth. The tempest, so long muttering in the West, had come upon him unexpectedly, for he had given all his attention to the spreading fire.

And now came the rain—no refreshing, sweet, saturating shower; but a thunderous, blinding fall of water that first set the burning woods to steaming and then drowned out every spark of fire on upland as well as lowland.

It was a cloudburst—a downpour such as Hiram had seldom experienced before. Exhausted, he lay on the bank and let the pelting rain soak him to the skin.

He did not care. Half drowned by the beating rain, he only crowed his delight at the downpour. Every spark of fire was flooded out. The danger was past.

He finally arose, and staggered through the downpour to the house, only happy that—by a merciful interposition of Providence—the peril had been overcome.

He tore off his clothing on the stoop, there in the pitch darkness, and crept up to his bedroom where he rubbed himself down with a crash-towel, and finally tumbled into bed and slept like a log till broad daylight.

CHAPTER XXII
FIRST FRUITS

For the first time since they had come to the farm, Hiram was the last to get up in the house. And when he came down to breakfast, still trembling from the exertion of the previous night, Mrs. Atterson screamed at the sight of him.

"For the good Land o' Goshen!" she cried. "You look like a singed chicken, Hiram Strong! Whatever have you been doing to yourself?"

He told them of the fight he had had while they slept. But he could talk about it jokingly now, although Sister was inclined to snivel a little over his danger.

"That Dickerson boy ought to be lashed—Nine and thirty lashes—none too much—This sausage is good—humph!—and pancakes—fit for the gods—But he'll come back—do more damage—the butter, yes I I want butter—and syrup, though two spreads is reckless extravagance—Eh? eh? can't prove anything against that Dickerson lout?-well, mebbe not."

So Old Lem Camp commented upon the affair. But Hiram could not prove that the neighbor's boy had done any of these things which pointed to a malicious enemy.

The young farmer began to wonder if he could not lay a trap, and so bring about his undoing.

As soon as the ground was in fit condition again (for the nights rain had been heavy) Hiram scattered the lime he had planned to use upon the four acres of land plowed for corn, and dragged it in with a spike-toothed harrow.

Working as he was with one horse alone, this took considerable time, and when this corn land was ready, it was time for him to go through the garden piece again with the horse cultivator.

Sister and Lem Camp, both, had learned to use the man-weight wheel-hoe, and the fine stuff was thinned and the weeds well cut out. From time to time the young farmer had planted peas—both the dwarf and taller varieties—and now he risked putting in some early beans—"snap" and bush limas—and his first planting of sweet corn.

Of the latter he put in four rows across the garden, each, of sixty-five day, seventy-five day, and ninety day sugar corn—all of well-known kinds. He planned later to put in, every fortnight, four rows of a mid-length season corn, so as to have green corn for sale, and for the house, up to frost.

The potatoes were growing finely and he hilled them up for the first time. He marked his four-acre lot for field corn—cross-checking it three-feet, ten inches apart. This made twenty-seven hundred and fifty hills to the acre, and with the hand-planter—an ingenious but cheap machine—he dropped two and three kernels to the hill.

This upland, save where he had spread coarse stable manure, was not rich. Upon each corn-hill he had Sister throw half a handful of fertilizer. She followed him as he used the planter, and they planted and fertilized the entire four acres in less than two days.

The lime he had put into the land would release such fertility as remained dormant there; but Hiram did not expect a big crop of corn on that piece. If he made two good ears to the hill he would be satisfied.

He had knocked together a rough cold-frame, on the sunny side of the woodshed, to fit some old sash he had found in the barn. Into the rich earth sifted to make the bed in this frame, he transplanted tomato, egg-plant, pepper and other plants of a delicate nature. Early cabbage and cauliflower had already gone into the garden plot, and in the midst of an early and saturating rain, all day long, he had transplanted table-beets into the rows he had marked out for them.

This variety of vegetables were now all growing finely. He sold nearly six dollars' worth of radishes in town, and these radishes he showed Mrs. Atterson were really "clear profit." They had all been pulled from the rows of carrots and other small seeds.

There were several heavy rains after the tempest which had been so Providential; the ground was well saturated, and the river had risen until it roared between its banks in a voice that could be heard, on a still day, at the house.

The rains started the vegetation growing by leaps and bounds; weeds always increase faster than any other growing thing.

There was plenty for Hiram to do in the garden, and he kept Sister and Old Lem Camp busy, too. They were at it from the first faint streak of light in the morning until dark.

But they were well—and happy. Mother Atterson, her heart troubled by thought of "that Pepper-man," could not always repress her smiles. If the danger of losing the farm were past, she would have had nothing in the world to trouble her.

The hundred eggs she had purchased for five dollars had proven more than sixty per cent fertile. Some advice that Hiram had given her enabled Mrs. Atterson to handle the chickens so that the loss from disease was very small.

He knocked together for her a couple of pens, eight feet square, which could be moved about on the grass every day. In these pens the seventy, or more, chicks thrived immensely. And Sister was devoted to them.

Meanwhile the old white-faced cow, that had been a terror to Mother Atterson at the start, had found her calf, and it was a heifer.

"Take my advice and raise it," said Hiram. "She is a scrub, but she is a pretty good scrub. You'll see that she will give a good measure of milk. And what this farm needs is cattle.

"If you could make stable manure enough to cover the cleared acres a foot deep, you could raise almost any crop you might name—and make money by it. The land is impoverished by the use of commercial fertilizers, unbalanced by humus."

"Well, I guess You know, Hiram," admitted Mrs. Atterson. "And that calf certainly is a pretty creeter. It would be too bad to turn it into veal."

Hiram did not intend to raise the calf expensively, however. He took it away from its mother right at the start, and in two weeks it was eating grass, and guzzling skimmed milk and calf-meal, while the old cow was beginning to show her employer her value.

Mrs. Atterson bought a small churn and quickly learned that "slight" at butter-making which is absolutely essential if one would succeed in the dairy business.

The cow turned out to pasture early in May, too; so her keep was not so heavy a burden. She lowed some after the calf; but the latter was growing finely under Hiram's care, and Mrs. Atterson had at least two pounds of butter for sale each week, and the housekeeper at the St. Beris school paid her thirty-five cents a pound for it.

Hiram gradually picked up a retail route in the town, which customers paid more for the surplus vegetables—and butter—than could be obtained at the stores. He had taught Sister how to drive, and sometimes even Mrs. Atterson went in with the vegetables.

This relieved the young farmer and allowed him to work in the fields. And during these warm, growing May days, he found plenty to do. Just as the field corn pushed through the ground he went into the lot with his 14-tooth harrow and broke up the crust and so killed the ever-springing weeds.

With the spikes on the harrow "set back," no corn-plants were dragged out of the ground. This first harrowing, too, mixed the fertilizer with the soil, and gave the corn the start it so sadly needed.

Busy as bees, the four transplanted people at the Atterson farmhouse accomplished a great deal during these first weeks of the warming season. And all four of them—Mrs. Atterson, Sister, Old Lem, and Hiram himself—enjoyed the work to the full.

CHAPTER XXIII
TOMATOES AND TROUBLE

Hiram Strong had decided that the market prospects of Scoville prophesied a good price for early tomatoes. He advised, therefore, a good sized patch of this vegetable.

He had planted in the window boxes seed of several different varieties. He had transplanted to the coldframe strong plants numbering nearly five hundred. He believed that, under garden cultivation, a tomato plant that would not yield fifty cents worth of fruit was not worth bothering with, while a dollar from a single plant was not beyond the bounds of probability.

It was safe, Hiram very well knew, to set out tomato plants in this locality much before the middle of May; yet he was willing to take some risks, and go to some trouble, for the sake of getting early ripened tomatoes into the Scoville market.

As Henry Pollock had prophesied, Hiram did not see much of his friend during corn-planting time. The Pollocks put nearly fifty acres in corn, and the whole family helped in the work, including Mrs. Pollock herself, and down to the child next to the baby. This little toddler amused his younger brother, and brought water to the field for the workers.

Other families in the neighborhood did the same, Hiram noticed. They all strained every effort to put in corn, cultivating as big a crop as they possibly could handle.

This was why locally grown vegetables were scarce in Scoville. And the young farmer proposed to take advantage of this condition of affairs to the best of his ability.

If they were only to remain here on the farm long enough to handle this one crop, Hiram determined to make that crop pay his employer as well as possible, although he, himself, had no share in such profit.

Henry Pollock, however, came along while Hiram was making ready his plat in the garden for tomatoes. The young farmer was setting several rows of two-inch thick stakes across the garden, sixteen feet apart in the row, the rows four feet apart. The stakes themselves were about four feet out of the ground.

"What ye doin' there, Hiram?" asked Henry, curiously. "Building a fence?"

"Not exactly."

"Ain't goin' to have a chicken run out here in the garden, be ye?"

"I should hope not! The chickens on this place will never mix with the garden trucks, if I have any say about it," declared Hiram, laughing.

"By Jo!" exclaimed Henry. "Dad says Maw's dratted hens eat up a couple hundred dollars' worth of corn and clover every year for him-runnin' loose as they do."

"Why doesn't he build your mother proper runs, then, plant green stuff in several yards, and change the flock over, from yard to yard?" "Oh, hens won't do well shut up; Maw says so," said Henry, repeating the lazy farmer's unfounded declaration-probably originated ages ago, when poultry was first domesticated.

"I'll show you, next year, if we are around here," said Hiram, "whether poultry will do well enclosed in yards."

"I told mother you didn't let your chickens run free, and had no hens with them," said Henry, thoughtfully.

"No. I do not believe in letting anything on a farm get into lazy habits. A hen is primarily intended to lay eggs. I send them back to work when they have hatched out their brood.

"Those home-made brooders of ours keep the chicks quite as warm, and never peck the little fellows, or step upon them, as the old hen often does."

"That's right, I allow," admitted Henry, grinning broadly.

"And some hens will traipse chicks through the grass and weeds as far as turkeys. No, sir! Send the hens back to business, and let the chicks shift for themselves. They'll do better."

"Them there in the pens certainly do look healthy," said his friend. "But you ain't said what you was doin' here, Hiram, setting these stakes?"

"Why, I'll tell you," returned Hiram. "This is my tomato patch."

"By Jo!" ejaculated Henry. "You don't want to set tomatoes so fur apart, do you?"

"No, no," laughed Hiram. "The posts are to string wires on. The tomatoes will be two feet apart in the row. As they grow I tie them to the wires, and so keep the fruit off the ground.

"The tomato ripens better and more evenly, and the fruit will come earlier, especially if I pinch back the ends of the vine from time to time, and remove some of the side branches."

"We don't do all that to raise a tomato crop. And we'll put in five acres for the cannery this year, as usual," said Henry, with some scorn.

"We run the rows out four feet apart, like you do, throwing up a list, in fact. Then father goes ahead with a stick, making a hole for the plant every three feet, so't they'll be check-rowed and we can cultivate them both ways—and we all set the plants.

"We never hand-hoe 'em—it don't pay. The cannery isn't giving but fifteen cents a basket this year—and it's got to be a full five-eighths basket, too, for they weigh 'em."

Hiram looked at him with a quizzical smile.

"So you set about thirty-six hundred and forty plants to the acre?" he said.

"I reckon so."

"And you'll have five acres of tomatoes?"

"Yep. So Dad says. He has contracted for that many. But our plants don't begin to be big enough to set out yet. We have to keep 'em covered nights."

"And I expect to have about five hundred plants in this patch," said Hiram, smiling. "I tell you what, Henry."

"Huh?" said the other boy. "I bet I take in from my patch—net income, I mean—this year as much as your father gets at the cannery for his whole crop."

"Nonsense!" cried Henry. "Maybe Dad'll make a hundred, or a hundred and twenty-five dollars. Sometimes tomatoes run as high as thirty dollars an acre around here."

"Wait and see," said Hiram, laughing. "It is going to cost me more to raise my crop, and market it, that's true. But if your father doesn't do better with his five acres than you say, I'll beat him."

"You can't do it, Hiram," cried Henry. "I can try, anyway," said Hiram, more quietly, but with confidence. "We'll see."

"And say," Henry added, suddenly, "I was going to tell you something. You won't raise these tomatoes—nor no other crop—if Pete Dickerson can stop ye."

"What's the matter with Pete now?" asked Hiram, troubled by thought of the secret enemy who had already struck at him in the dark.

"He was blowing about what he'd do to you down at the crossroads last evening," said Henry. "He and his father both hate you like poison, I expect.

"And the fellers down to Cale Schell's are always stirrin' up trouble. They think it is sport. Why, Pete got so mad last night he could ha' chewed tacks!"

"I have said nothing about Pete to anybody," said Hiram, firmly.

"That don't matter. They say you have. They tell Pete a whole lot of stuff just to see him git riled.

"And last night he slopped over. He said if you reported around that he put fire to Mis' Atterson's woods, he'd put it to the house and barns! Oh, he was wild."

Hiram's face flushed, and then paled.

"Did Pete try to bum the woods, Hiram?" queried Henry, shrewdly.

"I never even said I thought so to you, have I?" asked the young farmer, sternly.

"Nope. I only heard that fire got into the woods by accident, when I was in town. Somebody was hunting through there for coon, and saw the burned-over place. That's all the fellers at Cale's place knew, too, I reckon; but they jest put it up to Pete to mad him."

"And they succeeded, did they?" said Hiram, sternly.

"I reckon."

"Loose-mouthed people make more trouble in a community than downright mean ones," declared Hiram. "If I have any serious trouble with the Dickersons, like enough it will be because of the interference of the other neighbors."

"But," said Henry, preparing to go on, "Pete wouldn't dare fire your stable now—after sayin' he'd do it. He ain't quite so big a fool as all that."

But Hiram was not so sure. He had this additional trouble on his mind from this very hour, though he never said a word to Mrs. Atterson about it.

But every night before he went to bed be made around of the outbuildings to make sure that everything was right before he slept.

CHAPTER XXIV
"CORN THAT'S CORN"

Hiram caught sight of Pepper in town one day and went after him. He knew the real estate man had returned from his business trip, and the fact that the matter of the option was hanging fire, and troubling Mrs. Atterson exceedingly, urged Hiram go counter to Mr. Strickland's advice.

The lawyer had said: "Let sleeping dogs lie." Pepper had made no move, however, and the uncertainty was very trying both for the young farmer and his employer.

"How about that option you talked about, Mr. Pepper?" asked the "youth. Are you going to exercise it?"

"I've got time enough, ain't I?" returned the real estate man, eyeing Hiram in his very slyest way.

"I expect you have—if it really runs a year."

"You seen it, didn't you?" demanded Pepper.

"But we'd like Mr. Strickland to see it."

"He's goin' to act for Mrs. Atterson?" queried the man, with a scowl.

"Oh, yes."

"Well, he'll see it-when I'm ready to take it up. Don't you fret," retorted Pepper, and turned away.

This did not encourage the young farmer, nor was there anything in the man's manner to yield hope to Mrs. Atterson that she could feel secure in her title to the farm. So Hiram said nothing to her about meeting the man.

But the youth was very much puzzled. It really did seem as though Pepper was afraid to show that paper to Mr. Strickland.

"There's something queer about it, I believe," declared the youth to himself. "Somewhere there is a trick. He's afraid of being tripped up on it. But, why does he wait, if he knows the railroad is going to demand a strip of the farm and he can get a good price for it?

"Perhaps he is waiting to make sure that the railroad will condemn a piece of Mrs. Atterson's farm. If the board should change the route again, Pepper would have a farm on his hands that he might not be able to sell immediately at a profit.

"For we must confess, that sixteen hundred dollars, as farms have sold in the past around here, is a good price for the Atterson place. That's why Uncle Jeptha was willing to give an option for a month—if that was, in the beginning, the understanding the old man had of his agreement with Pepper.

"However, we might as well go ahead with the work, and take what comes to us in the end. I know no other way to do," quoth Hiram, with a sigh.

For he could not be very cheerful with the prospect of making only a single crop on the place. His profit was to have come out of the second year's crop—and, he felt, out of that bottom land which had so charmed him on the day he and Henry Pollock had gone over the Atterson Place.

Riches lay buried in that six acres of bottom. Hiram had read up on onion culture, and he believed that, if he planted his seed in hot beds, and transplanted the young onions to the rich soil in this bottom, he could raise fully as large onions as they did in either Texas or the Bermudas.

"Of course, they have the advantage of a longer season down there," thought Hiram, "and cheap labor. But maybe I can get cheap labor right around here. The children of these farmers are used to working in the fields. I ought to be able to get help pretty cheap.

"And when it comes to the market—why, I've got the Texas growers, at least, skinned a little! I can reach either the Philadelphia or New York market in a day. Yes; given the right conditions, onions ought to pay big down there on that lowland."

But this was not the only crop possibility be turned over in his mind. There were other vegetables that would grow luxuriantly on that bottom land—providing, always, the flood did not come and fulfill Henry Pollock's prophecy.

"Two feet of water on that meadow, eh?" thought Hiram. "Well, that certainly would be bad. I wouldn't want that to happen after the ground was plowed this year, even. It would tear up the land, and sour it, and spoil it for a corn-crop, indeed."

So he was down a good deal to the river's edge, watching the ebb and flow of the stream. A heavy rain would, over night, fill the river to its very brim and the open field, even beyond the marshy spot, would be a-slop with standing water.

"It sure wouldn't grow alfalfa," chuckled Hiram to himself one day. "For the water rises here a good deal closer to the surface than four feet, and alfalfa farmers declare that if the springs rise that high, there is no use in putting in alfalfa. Why! I reckon just now the water is within four inches of the top of the ground."

If the river remained so high, and the low ground so saturated with water, he knew, too, that he could not get the six acres plowed in time to put in corn this year. And it was this year's crop he must think about first.

Even if Pepper did not exercise his option, and turn Mrs. Atterson out of the place, a big commercial crop of onions, or any other better-paying crop, could only be tried the second year.

Hiram had got his seed corn for the upland piece of the man who raised the best corn in the community. He had tried the fertility of each ear, discarded those which proved weakly, or infertile, and his stand of corn for the four acres, which was now half hand high, was the best of any farmer between the Atterson place and town.

But this corn was a hundred-and-ten-day variety. The farmer he got it of told him that he had raised a crop from a piece planted the day before the Fourth of July; but it was safer to get it in at least by June fifteenth.

And here it was past June first, and the meadow land had not yet been plowed.

"However," Hiram said to Henry, when they walked down to the riverside on Sunday afternoon, "I'm going ahead on Faith—just as the minister said in church this morning. If Faith can move mountains, we'll give it a chance to move something right down here."

"I dunno, Hiram," returned the other boy, shaking his head. "Father says he'll git in here for you with three head and a Number 3 plow by the middle of this week if you say so—'nless it rains again, of course. But he's afeared you're goin' to waste Mrs. Atterson's money for her."

"Nothing ventured, nothing gained," quoted Hiram, grimly. "If a farmer didn't take chances every year, the whole world would starve to death!"

"Well," returned Henry, smiling too, "let the other fellow take the chances—that's dad's motter."

"Yes. And the 'chancey' fellow skims the cream of things every time. No, sir!" declared the young fellow, "I'm going to be among the cream-skimmers, or I won't be a farmer at all."

So the plow was put into the bottom-land Wednesday—and put in deep. By Friday night the whole piece was plowed and partly harrowed.

Hiram had drawn lime for this bottom-land, proposing to use beside only a small amount of fertilizer. He spread this lime from his one-horse wagon, while Henry drag-harrowed behind him, and by Saturday noon the job was done.

The horses had not mired at all, much to Mr. Pollock's surprise. And the plow had bit deep. All the heavy sod of the piece was covered well, and the seed bed was fairly level—for corn.

Although the Pollocks did not work on Saturday afternoon, Hiram did not feel as though he could stop at this time. Most of the farmers had already planted their last piece of corn. Monday would be the fifteenth of the month.

So the young farmer got his home-made corn-row marker down to the river-bottom and began marking the piece that afternoon.

This marker ran out three rows at each trip across the field, and with a white stake at either end, the youth managed to run his rows very straight. He had a good eye.

In this case he did not check-row his field. The land was rich—phenomenally rich, he believed. If he was going to have a crop of corn here, he wanted a crop worth while.

On the uplands the farmers were satisfied with from thirty to fifty baskets of ear-corn to the acre. If this lowland was what he believed it was, Hiram was sure it would make twice that.

And at that his corn crop here would only average twenty-five dollars to the acre—not a phenomenal profit for Mrs. Atterson in that.

But the land would be getting into shape for a better crop, and although corn is a crop that will soon impoverish ground, if planted year after year on the same piece, Hiram knew that the humus in this soil on the lowland was almost inexhaustible.

So he marked his rows the long way of the field—running with the river.

One of the implements left by Uncle Jeptha had been a one-horse corn-planter with a fertilizer attachment. Hiram used this, dropping two or three grains twenty-four inches apart, and setting the fertilizer attachment to one hundred and fifty pounds to the acre.

He was until the next Wednesday night planting the piece. Meanwhile it had not rained, and the river continued to recede. It was now almost as low as it had been the day Lettie Bronson's boating party had been "wrecked" under the big sycamore.

Hiram had not seen the Bronsons for some weeks, but about the time he got his late corn planted, Mr. Bronson drove into the Atterson yard, and found Hiram cultivating his first corn with the five-tooth cultivator.

"Well, well, Hiram!" exclaimed the Westerner, looking with a broad smile over the field. "That's as pretty a field of corn as I ever saw. I don't believe there is a hill missing."

"Only a few on the far edge, where the moles have been at work."

"Moles don't eat corn, Hiram."

"So they say," returned the young farmer, quietly. "I never could make up my mind about it.

"I'm sure, however, that if they are only after slugs and worms which are drawn to the corn hills by the commercial fertilizer, the moles do fully as much damage as the slugs would.

"You see, they make a cavity under the corn hill, and the roots of the plant wither. Excuse me, but I'd rather have Mr. Mole in somebody else's garden."

Mr. Bronson laughed. "Well, what the little gray fellows eat won't kill us. But they do spoil otherwise handsome rows. How did you get such a good stand of corn, Hiram?"

"I tested the seed in a seed box early in the spring. I wouldn't plant corn any other way. Aside from the hills the moles have spoiled, and a few an old crow pulled up, I've got no re-planting to do.

"And replanted hills are always behind the crop, and seldom make anything but fodder. If it wasn't for the look of the field, I'd never re-plant a hill of corn.

"Of course, I've got to thin this—two grains in the hill is enough on this land."

Mr. Bronson looked at him with growing surprise.

"Why, my boy, you talk just as though you had tilled the ground for a score of years. Who taught you so much about farming?"

"One of the best farmers who ever lived," said Hiram, with a smile. "My father. And he taught me to go to the correct sources for information, too."

"I believe you!" exclaimed Mr. Bronson. "And you're going to have 'corn that's corn', as we say in my part of the country, on this piece of land."

"Wait!" said Hiram, smiling and shaking his head.

"Wait for what?"

"Wait till you see the corn on my bottom-land—if the river down there doesn't drown it out. If we don't have too much rain, I'm going to have corn on that river-bottom that will beat anything in this county, Mr. Bronson."

And the young farmer spoke with assurance.

CHAPTER XXV
THE BARBECUE

On the seventeenth day of June Hiram had "grappled out" a mess of potatoes for their dinner. They were larger than hen's eggs and came upon the table mealy and white.

Potatoes were selling at retail in Scoville for two dollars the bushel. Before the end of that week—after the lowland corn was planted—Hiram dug two rows of potatoes, sorted them, and carted them to town, together with some bunched beets, a few bunches of young carrots, radishes and salad.

The potatoes he sold for fifty cents the five-eighth basket, from house to house, and he brought back, for his load of vegetables, ten dollars and twenty cents, which he handed to Mrs. Atterson, much to that lady's joy.

"My soul and body, Hiram!" she exclaimed. "This is just a God-send— no less. Do you know that we've sold nigh twenty-five dollars' worth of stuff already this spring, besides that pair of pigs I let Pollock have, and the butter to St. Beris?"

"And it's only a beginning," Hiram told her. "Wait til' the peas come along—we'll have a mess for the table in a few days now. And the sweet corn and tomatoes.

"If you and Sister can do the selling, it will help out a whole lot, of course. I wish we had another horse."

"Or an automobile," said Sister, clapping her hands. "Wouldn't it be fine to run into town in an auto, with a lot of vegetables? Then Hiram could keep right at work with the horse and not have to stop to harness up for us."

"Shucks, child!" admonished Mrs. Atterson. "What big idees you do get in that noddle o' yourn."

The girls' boarding school and the two hotels proved good customers for Hiram's early vegetables; for nobody around Scoville had potatoes at this time, and Hiram's early peas were two weeks ahead of other people's.

Having got a certain number of towns folks to expect him at least thrice a week, when other farmers had green stuff for sale they could not easily "cut out" Hiram later in the season.

And not always did the young farmer have to leave his work at home to deliver the vegetables and Mrs. Atterson's butter. Sister, or the old lady herself, could go to town if the load was not too heavy.

Of course, it cost considerable to live. And hogfood and grain for the horse and cow had to be bought. Hiram was fattening four of the spring shoats against winter. Two they could sell and two kill for their own use.

"Goin' to be big doin's on the Fourth this year, Hiram," said Henry Pollock, meeting the young farmer on the road from town one day. "Heard about it?"

"In Scoville, do you mean? They're going to have a 'Safe and Sane' Fourth, the Banner says."

"Nope. We don't think much of goin' to town Fourth of July. And this year there's goin' to be a big picnic in Langdon's Grove—that's up the river, you know."

"A public picnic?"

"Sure. A barbecue, we call it," said Henry. "We have one at the Grove ev'ry year. This time the two Sunday Schools is goin' to join and have a big time. You and Sister don't want to miss it. That Mr. Bronson's goin' to give a whole side o' beef, they tell me, to roast over the fires."

"A big banquet is in prospect, is it?" asked Hiram, smiling.

"And a stew! Gee! you never eat one o' these barbecue stews, did ye? Some of us will go huntin' the day before, and there'll be birds, and squirrels, as well as chickens in that stew—and lima beans, and corn, and everything good you can think of!" and Henry smacked his lips in prospect.

Then he added, bethinking himself of his errand:

"Everybody chips in and gives the things to eat. What'll you give, Hiram?"

"Some vegetables," said Hiram, quickly. "Mrs. Atterson won't object, I guess. Do they want tomatoes for their stew?"

"Won't be no tomatoes ripe, Hiram," said Henry, decidedly.

"There won't, eh? You come out and take a look at mine," said Hiram, laughing.

Of all the rows of vegetables in Hiram's garden plot, the thriftiest and handsomest were the trellised tomato plants. It took nearly half of Sister's time to keep the plants tied up and pinched back, as Hiram had taught her.

But the stalks were already heavily laden with fruit; and those hanging lowest on the sturdy vines were already blushing.

"By Jo!" gasped Henry. "You've done it, ain't you? But the cannery won't take 'em yet awhile—and they'll all be gone before September."

"The cannery won't get many of my tomatoes," laughed Hiram. "And these vines properly trained and cultivated as they are, will bear fruit up to frost. You wait and see."

"I'll have to tell dad to come and look at these. I dunno, Hiram, if you can sell 'em at retail, but you'll git as much for 'em as dad does for his whole crop—just as you said."

"That's what I'm aiming for," responded Hiram. "But would the ladies who cook the barbecue stew care for tomatoes, do you think?"

"We never git tomatoes this early," said Henry. "How about potatoes? And there ain't many folks dug any of theirn yet, but you."

So, after speaking with Mrs. Atterson, Hiram agreed to supply a barrel of potatoes for the barbecue, and the day before the Fourth, one of the farmers came with a wagon to pick up the supplies.

Everybody at the Atterson farm would go to the grove—that was understood.

"If one knocks off work, the others can," declared Mother Atterson. "You see that things is left all right for the critters, Hiram, and we'll tend to things indoors so that we can be gone till night."

"And do, Hiram, look out for my poults the last thing," cried Sister.

Mrs. Larriper had given Sister a setting of ten turkey eggs and every one of them had hatched under one of Mrs. Atterson's motherly old hens. At first the girl had kept the young turkeys and their foster mother right near the house, so that she could watch them carefully.

But poults are rangy, and these being particularly strong and thrifty, they soon ran the old hen pretty nearly to death.

So Hiram had built a coop into which they could go at night, safe from any vermin, and set it far down in the east lot, near the woods. Sister usually went down with a little grain twice a day to call them up, and keep them tame.

"But when they get big enough to roost in the fall, I expect we'll have to gather that crop with a gun," Hiram told her, laughing.

Many of the farmers teams were strung out along the road long before Hiram was ready to set out. He had made sure that the spring wagon was in good shape, and he had built an extra seat for it, so that the four rode very comfortably.

Like every other Fourth of July, the sun was broiling hot! And the dust rose in clouds as the faster teams passed their slow old nag.

Mrs. Atterson sat up very primly in her best silk, holding a parasol and wearing a pair of lace mits that had appeared on state occasions for the past twenty years, at least.

Sister was growing like a weed, and it was hard to keep her skirts and sleeves at a proper length. But she was an entirely different looking girl from the boarding house slavey whom Hiram remembered so keenly back in Crawberry.

As for Old Lem Camp, he was as cheerful as Hiram had ever seen him, and showed a deal of interest in everything about the farm, and had proved himself, as Mrs. Atterson had prophesied, a great help.

Scarcely a house along the road was not shut up and the dooryard deserted—for everybody was going to the barbecue. All but the Dickerson family. Sam was at work in the fields, and the haggard Mrs. Dickerson looked dumbly from her porch, with a crying baby in her scrawny arms as the Attersons and Hiram passed.

But Pete was at the barbecue. He was there when Hiram arrived, and he was making himself quite as prominent as anybody.

Indeed, he made himself so obnoxious finally, that one of the rough men who was keeping up the fires threatened to chuck Pete into the biggest one, and then cool him off in the river.

Otherwise, however, the barbecue passed off very pleasantly. The men who governed it saw that no liquor was brought along, and the unruly element to which Pete belonged was kept under with an iron hand.

There was so little "fun", of a kind, in Pete's estimation that, after the big event of the day—the banquet—he and some of his friends disappeared. And the picnicking ground was a much quieter and pleasanter place after their departure.

The newcomers into the community made many friends and acquaintances that day. Sister was going to school in the fall, and she found many girls of her age whom she would meet there.

Mrs. Atterson met the older ladies, and was invited to join no less than two "Ladies' Aids", and, as she said, "if she called on all the folks she'd agreed to visit, she'd be goin' ev'ry day from then till Christmas!"

As for Hiram, the men and older boys were rather inclined to jolly him a bit. Not many of them had been upon the Atterson place to see what he had done, but they had heard some stories of his proposed crops that amused them.

When Mr. Bronson, however, whom the local men knew to be a big farmer in the Middle West, and who owned many farms out there now, spoke favorably of Hiram's work, the local men listened respectfully.

"The boy's got it in him to do something," the Westerner said, in his hearty fashion. "You're eating his potatoes now, I understand. Which one of you can dig early potatoes like those?

"And he's got the best stand of corn in the county."

"On that river-bottom, you mean?" asked one.

"And on the upland, too. You fellows want to look about you a little. Most of you don't see beyond the end of your noses. You watch out, or Hiram Strong is going to beat every last one of you this year—and that's a run-down farm he's got, at that."

CHAPTER XXVI
SISTER'S TURKEYS

But Lettie was not at the barbecue, and to tell the truth, Hiram Strong was disappointed.

Despite the fact that she had seemed inclined to snub him, the young farmer was vastly taken with the pretty girl. He had seen nobody about Scoville as attractive as Lettie—nor anywhere else, for that matter!

He was too proud to call at the Bronson place, although Mr. Bronson invited him whenever he saw Hiram. And at first, Lettie had asked him to come, too.

But the Western girl did not like being thwarted in any matter—even the smallest. And when Hiram would not come to take Pete Dickerson's place, the very much indulged girl had showed the young farmer that she was offended.

However, the afternoon at Langdon's Grove passed very pleasantly, and Hiram and his party did not arrive at the farm again until dusk had fallen.

"I'll go down and shut your turkeys up for the night, Sister," Hiram said, after he had done the other chores for he knew the girl would be afraid to go so far from the house by lantern-light.

And when he reached the turkey coop, 'way down in the field, Hiram was very glad indeed that he had come instead of the girl.

For the coop was empty. There wasn't a turkey inside, or thereabout. It had been dark an hour and more, then, and the poults should long since have been hovered in the coop.

Had some marauding fox, or other "varmint", run the young turkeys off their reservation? That seemed improbable at this time of year—and so early in the evening. Foxes do not usually go hunting before midnight, nor do other predatory animals.

Hiram had brought the barn lantern with him, and he took a look around the neighborhood of the empty coop.

"My goodness!" he mused, "Sister will cry her eyes out if anything's happened to those little turks. Now, what's this?"

The ground was cut up at a little distance from the coop. He examined the tracks closely.

They were fresh—very fresh indeed. The wheel tracks of a light wagon showed, and the prints of a horse's shod hoofs.

The wagon had been driven down from the main road, and had turned sharply here by the coop. Hiram knew, too, that it had stood there for some time, for the horse had moved uneasily.

Of course, that proved the driver had gotten out of the wagon and left the horse alone. Doubtless there was but one thief—for it was positive that the turkeys had been removed by a two-footed—not a four-footed—marauder.

"And who would be mean enough to steal Sister's turkeys? Almost everybody in the neighborhood has a few to fatten for Thanksgiving and Christmas. Who—did—this?"

He followed the wheel marks of the wagon to the road. He saw the track where it turned into the field, and where it turned out again. And it showed plainly that the thief came from town, and returned in that direction.

Of course, in the roadway it was impossible to trace the particular tracks made by the thief's horse and wagon. Too many other vehicles had been over the road within the past hour.

The thief must have driven into the field just after night-fall, plucked the ten young turkeys, one by one, out of the coop, tying their feet and flinging them into the bottom of his wagon. Covered with a bag, the frightened turkeys would never utter a peep while it remained dark.

"I hate to tell Sister—I can't tell her," Hiram said, as he went slowly back to the house. For Sister had been "counting chickens" again, and she had figured that, at eighteen cents per pound, live weight, the ten turkeys would pay for all the clothes she would need that winter, and give her "Christmas money", too.

The young farmer shrank from meeting the girl again that night, and he delayed going into the house as long as possible. Then he found they had all retired, leaving him a cold supper at the end of the kitchen table.

The disappearance of the turkeys kept Hiram tossing, wakeful, upon his bed for some hours. He could not fail to connect this robbery with the other things that had been done, during the past weeks, to injure those living at the Atterson farm.

Was the secret enemy really Peter Dickerson? And had Pete committed this crime now?

Yet the horse and wagon had come from the direction opposite the Dickerson farm, and had returned as it came.

"I don't know whether I am accusing that fellow wrongfully, or not," muttered Hiram, at last. "But I am going to find out. Sister isn't going to lose her turkeys without my doing everything in my power to get them back and punish the thief."

He usually arose in the morning before anybody else was astir, so it was easy for Hiram to slip out of the house and down to the field to the empty turkey coop.

The marks of horse and wagon were quite as plain in the faint light of dawn as they had been the night before. In the darkness the thief had driven his wagon over some small stumps, amid which his horse had scrambled in some difficulty, it was plain.

Hiram, tracing out these marks as a Red Indian follows a trail, saw something upon the edge of one of the half-decayed stumps that interested him greatly.

He stood up the next moment with this clue in his hand—a white, coarse hair, perhaps four inches in length.

"That was scraped off the horse's fetlock as he scrambled over this stump," muttered Hiram. "Now, who drives a white horse, or a horse with white feet, in this neighborhood?"

"Can I narrow the search down in this way, I wonder?" and for some moments the youth stood there, in the growing light of early morning, canvassing the subject from that angle.

CHAPTER XXVII
RUN TO EARTH

A broad streak of crimson along the eastern horizon, over the treetops, announced the coming of the sun when Hiram Strong reached the automobile road to which he, on the previous night, had traced the thief that had stolen Sister's poults.

Now he looked at the track again. It surely had come from the direction of Scoville, and it turned back that way.

Yet he looked at the white horse-hair scraped off upon the stump, and he turned his back upon these signs and strode along the road toward his own home.

Smoke was just curling from the Atterson chimney; Sister, or Mrs. Atterson, was just building the fire. But they did not see Hiram as he went by.

Hiram's quest led him past the place and to the Dickerson farm. There nobody was yet astir, save the mules and horses in the barnyard, who called as he went by, hoping for their breakfast.

Hiram knew that the Dickersons had turkeys and, like most of the other farmers, cooped them in distant fields away from the house. He found three coops in the middle of an old oat-field tinder a spreading beech.

The old turks roosted upon the limbs of the beech at night; they were already up and away, hunting grasshoppers for breakfast. But quite a few poults were running and peeping about the coops, with two hen turkeys playing guard to them.

Hiram saw where a wagon had been driven in here, and turned, too. The tracks were made recently. And one of the coops was shut tight, although he knew by the rustling within that there were young turkeys in it.

It was too dark within the hutch, however, for the youth to number the poults confined there.

He strolled back across the fields to the rear of the Dickerson house. Passing the barnyard first, he halted and examined the bright bay horse, with white feet—the one that Pete had driven to the barbecue the day before—the only one Pete was ever allowed to drive off the farm.

The Dickersons, father and son, were not as early risers as most farmers in those parts. At least, they were not up betimes on this morning.

But Mrs. Dickerson had built the fire now and was stirring about the porch when Hiram arrived at the step, filling her kettle at the pump.

"Mornin', Mr. Strong," she said, in her startled way, eyeing Hiram askance.

She was a lean, sharp-featured woman, with a hopeless droop to her shoulders.

"Good-morning, Mrs. Dickerson," said Hiram, gravely. "How many young turkeys have you this year?"

The woman shrank back and almost dropped the kettle she had filled to the pump-bench. Her eyes glared.

Somewhere in the house a baby squatted; then a door banged and Hiram heard Dickerson's heavy step descending the stair.

"You have a coop of poults down there, Mrs. Dickerson," continued Hiram, confidently, "that I know belongs to us. I traced Pete's tracks with the wagon and the white-footed horse. Now, this is going to make trouble for Pete——"

"What's the matter with Pete, now?" demanded Dickerson's harsh voice, and he came out upon the porch.

He scowled at sight of Hiram, and continued:

"What are you roaming around here for, Strong? Can't you keep on your own side of the fence?"

"It's little I'll ever trouble you, Mr. Dickerson," said Hiram, "sharply, if you and yours don't trouble me, I can assure you."

"What's eating you now?" demanded the man, roughly.

"Why, I'll tell you, Mr. Dickerson," said Hiram, quickly. "Somebody's stolen our turkeys—ten of them. And I have found them down there where your turkeys roost. The natural inference is that somebody here knows about it——"

Dickerson—just out of his bed and as ugly as many people are when they first get up—leaped for the young farmer from the porch, and had him in his grip before Hiram could help himself.

The woman screamed. There was a racket in the house, for some of the children had been watching from the window. "Dad's goin' to lick him!" squalled one of the girls.

"You come here and intermate that any of my family's thieves, do you?" the angry man roared.

"Stop that, Sam Dickerson!" cried his wife. She suddenly gained courage and ran to the struggling pair, and tried to haul Sam away from Hiram.

"The boy's right," she gasped. "I heard Pete tellin' little Sam last night what he'd done. It's come to a pretty pass, so it has, if you are goin' to uphold that bad boy in thieving——"

"Hush up, Maw!" cried Pete's voice from the house.

"Come out here, you scalawag!" ordered his father, relaxing his hold on Hiram.

Pete slouched out on the porch, wearing a grin that was half sheepish, half worried.

"What's this Strong says about turkeys?" demanded Sam Dickerson, sternly.

"'Tain't so!" declared Pete. "I ain't seen no turkeys."

"I have found them," said Hiram, quietly. "And the coopful is down yonder in your lot. You thought to fool me by turning into our farm from the direction of Scoville, and driving back that way; but you turned around in the road under that overhanging oak, where I picked Lettie Bronson off the back of the runaway horse last Spring.

"Now, those ten turkeys belong to Sister. She'll be heart-broken if anything happens to them. You have played me several mean tricks since I have been here, Pete Dickerson——"

"No, I ain't!" interrupted the boy.

"Who took the burr off the end of my axle and let me down in the road that night?" demanded Hiram, his rage rising.

Pete could not forbear a grin at this remembrance.

"And who tampered with our pump the next morning? And who watched and waited till we left the lower meadow that night we burned the rubbish, and then set fire to our woods——"

Mrs. Dickerson screamed again. "I knew that fire never come by accident," she moaned.

"You shut up, Maw!" admonished her hopeful son again.

"And now, I've got you," declared Hiram, with confidence. "I can tell those ten poults. I marked them for Sister long ago so that, if they went to the neighbors, they could be easily identified.

"They're in that shut-up coop down yonder," continued Hiram, "and unless you agree to bring them back at once, and put them in our coop, I shall hitch up and go to town, first thing, and get out a warrant for your arrest."

Sam had remained silent for a minute, or two. Now he said, decidedly:

"You needn't threaten no more, young feller. I can see plain enough that Pete's been carrying his fun too far— —"

"Fun!" ejaculated Hiram.

"That's what I said," growled Sam. "He'll bring the turkeys back-and before he has his breakfast, too."

"All right," said Hiram, knowing full well that there was nothing to be made by quarreling with Sam Dickerson. "His returning the turkeys, however, will not keep me from speaking to the constable the very next time Pete plays any of his tricks around our place.

"It may be 'fun' for him; but it won't look so funny from the inside of the town jail."

He walked off after this threat. And he was sorry he had said it. For he had no real intention of having Pete arrested, and an empty threat is of no use to anybody.

The turkeys came back; Sister did not even know that they had been stolen, for when she went down to feed them about the middle of the forenoon, all ten came running to her call.

But Pete Dickerson ceased from troubling for a time, much to Hiram's satisfaction.

Meanwhile the crops were coming on finely. Hiram's tomatoes were bringing good prices in Scoville, and as he had such a quantity and was so much earlier than the other farmers around about, he did, as he told Henry he would do, "skim the cream off the market."

He bought some crates and baskets in town, too, and shipped some of the tomatoes to a produce man he knew in Crawberry—a man whom he could trust to treat him fairly. During the season that man's checks to Mrs. Atterson amounted to fifty-four dollars.

Three times a week the spring wagon went to town with vegetables for the school, the hotels, and their retail customers. The whole family worked long hours, and worked hard; but nobody complained.

No rain fell of any consequence until the latter part of July; and then there was no danger of the river overflowing and drowning out the corn.

And that corn! By the last of July it was waist high, growing rank and strong, and of that black-green color which delights the farmer's eye.

Mr. Bronson walked down to the river especially to see it. Like Hiram's upland corn, there was scarcely a hill missing, save where the muskrats had dug in from the river bank and disturbed the corn hills.

"That's the finest-looking corn in this county, bar none, Hiram," declared Bronson. "I have seldom seen better looking in the rich bottom-lands of the West. And you certainly do keep it clean, boy."

"No use in putting in a crop if you don't 'tend it," said the young farmer, sententiously.

"And what's this along here?" asked the gentleman, pointing to a row or two of small stuff along the inner edge of the field.

"I'm trying onions and celery down here. I want to put a commercial crop into this field next year—if we are let stay here—that will pay Mrs. Atterson and me a real profit," and Hiram laughed.

"What do you call a real profit?" inquired Mr. Bronson, seriously.

"Four hundred dollars an acre, net," said the young farmer, promptly.

"Why, Hiram, you can't do that!" cried the gentleman.

"It's being done—in other localities and on soil not so rich as this—and I believe I can do it."

"With onions or celery?" "Yes, sir." "Which—or both?" asked the Westerner, interested.

"I am trying them out here, as you see. I believe it will be celery. This soil is naturally wet, and celery is a glutton for water. Then, it is a late piece, and celery should be transplanted twice before it is put in the field, I believe."

"A lot of work, boy," said Mr. Bronson, shaking his head.

"Well, I never expect to get something for nothing," remarked Hiram.

"And how about the onions?"

"Why, they don't seem to do so well. There is something lacking in the land to make them do their best. I believe it is too cold. And, then, I am watching the onion market, and I am afraid that too many people have gone into the game in certain sections, and are bound to create an over-supply."

The gentleman looked at him curiously.

"You certainly are an able-minded youngster, Hiram," he observed. "I s'pose if you do so well here next year as you expect, a charge of dynamite wouldn't blast you away from the Atterson farm?"

"Why, Mr. Bronson," responded the young farmer, "I don't want to run a one-horse farm all my life. And this never can be much more. It isn't near enough to any big city to be a real truck farm—and I'm interested in bigger things.

"No, sir. The Atterson Eighty is only a stepping stone for me. I hope I'll go higher before long."

CHAPTER XXVIII
HARVEST

But Hiram was not at all sure that he would ever see a celery crop in this bottom-land. Pepper still "hung fire" and he would not go to Mr. Strickland with his option.

"I don't hafter," he told Hiram. "When I git ready I'll let ye know, be sure o' that."

The fact was that the railroad had made no further move. Mr. Strickland admitted to Mrs. Atterson that if the strip along the east boundary of the farm was condemned by the railroad, she ought to get a thousand dollars for it.

"But if the railroad board should change its mind again," added the lawyer, "sixteen hundred dollars would not be a speculative price to pay for your farm—and well Pepper knows it."

"Then Mr. Damocles's sword has got to hang over us, has it?" demanded the old lady.

"I am afraid so," admitted the lawyer, smiling.

Mrs. Atterson could not be more troubled than was Hiram himself. Youth feels the sting of such arrows of fortune more keenly than does age. We get "case-hardened" to trouble as the years bend our shoulders.

The thought that he might, after all, get nothing but a hundred dollars and his board for all the work he had done in preparation for the second year's crop sometimes embittered Hiram's thoughts.

Once, when he spoke to Pepper, and the snaky man sneered at him and laughed, the young farmer came near attacking him then and there in the street.

"I certainly could have given that Pepper as good a thrashing as ever he got," muttered Hiram. "And even Pete Dickerson never deserved one more than Pepper."

Pete fought shy of Hiram these days, and as the summer waned the young farmer gradually became less watchful and expectant of trouble from the direction of the west boundary of the Atterson Eighty.

But there was little breathing spell for him in the work of the farm.

"When we lay by the corn, you bet dad an' me goes fishing!" Henry Pollock told Hiram, one day.

But it wasn't often that the young farmer could take half a day off for any such pleasure.

"You've bit off more'n you kin chaw," observed Henry.

"That's all right; I'll keep chewing at it, just the same," returned Hiram cheerfully.

For the truck crop was bringing them in a bigger sum of money than even Hiram had expected. The season had been very favorable, indeed; Hiram's vegetables had come along in good time, and even the barrels of sweet corn he shipped to Crawberry brought a fair price—much better than he could have got at the local cannery.

When the tomato pack came on, however, he did sell many baskets of his "seconds" to the cannery. But the selected tomatoes he continued to ship to Crawberry, and having established a reputation with his produce man for handsome and evenly ripened fruit, the prices received were good all through the season.

He saw the sum for tomatoes pass the hundred and fifty dollar mark before frost struck the vines. Even then he was not satisfied. There was a small cellar under the Atterson house, and when the frosty nights of October came, Hiram dragged up the vines still bearing fruit, by the roots, and hung them in the cellar, where the tomatoes continued to ripen slowly nearly up to Thanksgiving.

Other crops did almost as well in proportion. He had put in no late potatoes; but in September he harvested the balance of his early crop and, as they were a good keeping variety, he knew there would be enough to keep the family supplied until the next season.

Of other roots, including a patch of well-grown mangels for Mrs. Atterson's handsome flock of chickens, there were plenty to carry the family over the winter.

As the frosts became harder Hiram dug his root pits in the high, light soil of the garden, drew pinetags to cover them, and, gradually, as the winter advanced, heaped the earth over the various piles of roots to keep them through the winter.

Meanwhile, in September, corn harvest had come on. The four acres Hiram had planted below the stables yielded a fair crop, that part of the land he had been able to enrich with coarse manure showing a much better average than the remainder.

The four acres yielded them something over one hundred and sixty baskets of sound corn which, as corn was then selling for fifty cents per bushel, meant that the crop was worth about forty dollars.

As near as Hiram could figure it had cost about fifteen dollars to raise the crop; therefore the profit to Mrs. Atterson was some twenty-five dollars.

Besides the profit from some of the garden crops, this was very small indeed; as Hiram said, it did not pay well enough to plant small patches of corn for them to fool with it much.

"The only way to make a good profit out of corn corn a place like this," he said to Henry, who would not be convinced, "is to have a big drove of hogs and turn them into the field to fatten on the standing corn."

"But that would be wasteful!" cried Henry, shocked at the suggestion.

"Big pork producers do not find it so," returned Hiram, confidently. "Or else one wants a drove of cattle to fatten, and cuts the corn green and shreds it, blowing it into a silo.

"The idea is to get the cost of the corn crop back through the price paid by the butcher for your stock, or hogs."

"Nobody ever did that around here," declared young Pollock.

"And that's why nobody gets ahead very fast around here. Henry, why don't you strike out and do something new—just to surprise 'em?

"Stop selling a little tad of this, and a little tad of that off the farm and stick to the good farmer's rule: 'Never sell anything off the place that can't walk off.'"

"I've heard that before," said Henry, sighing.

"And even then just so much fertility goes with every yoke of steers or pair of fat hogs. But it is less loss, in proportion, than when the corn, or oats, or wheat itself is sold."

CHAPTER XXIX
LETTIE BRONSON'S CORN HUSKING

Sister had begun school on the very first day it opened—in September. She was delighted, for although she had had "lessons" at the "institution", they had not been like this regular attendance, with other free and happy children, at a good country school.

Sister was growing not alone in body, but in mind. And the improvement in her appearance was something marvelous.

"It certainly does astonish me, every time I think o' that youngun and the way she looked when she come to me from the charity school," declared Mother Atterson.

"Who'd want a better lookin' young'un now? She'd be the pride of any mother's heart, she'd be.

"If there's folks belongin' to her, and they have neglected her all these years, in my opinion they're lackin' in sense, Hiram."

"They certainly have been lacking in the milk of human kindness," admitted the young farmer.

"Huh! That milk's easily soured in many folks," responded Mrs. Atterson. "But Sister's folks, whoever they be, will be sorry some day."

"You don't suppose she really has any family, do you?" demanded Hiram.

"No father nor mother, I expect. But many a family will get rid of a young'un too small to be of any use, when they probably have many children of their own.

"And if there was a little bait of money coming to the child, as that lawyer told the institution matron, that would be another reason for losing her in this great world."

"I'm afraid Sister will never find her folks, Mrs. Atterson," said Hiram, shaking his head.

"Huh! If she don't, it's no loss to her. It's loss to them," declared the old lady. "And I'd hate to have anybody come and take her away from us now."

Sister no longer wore her short hair in four "pigtails". She had learned to dress it neatly like other girls of her age, and although it would never be like the beautiful blue-black tresses of Lettie Bronson, Hiram had to admit that the soft brown of Sister's hair, waving so prettily over her forehead, made the girl's features more than a little attractive.

She was an entirely different person, too, from the one who had helped Lettie and her friends ashore from the grounded motor-boat that day, so long ago—and so Lettie herself thought when she rode into the Atterson yard one October day on her bay horse, and Sister met her on the porch.

"Why, you're Mrs. Atterson's girl, aren't you?" cried Lettie, leaning from her saddle to offer her hand to Sister. "I wouldn't have known you."

Sister was getting plump, she had roses in her cheeks, and she wore a neat, whole, and becoming dress.

"You're Miss Bronson," said Sister, gravely. "I wouldn't forget you."

Perhaps there was something in what Sister said that stung Lettie Bronson's memory. She flushed a little; but then she smiled most charmingly and asked for Hiram.

"Husking corn, Miss, with Henry Pollock, down on the bottom-land."

"Oh! way down there? Well! you tell him—Why, I'll want you to come, too," laughed Lettie, quite at her best now.

Nobody could fail to answer Lettie Bronson's smile with its reflection, when she chose to exert herself in that direction.

"Why, I just came to tell you both that on Friday we're going to have an old-fashioned husking-bee for all the young folks of the neighborhood, at our place. You must come yourself—er—Sister, and tell Hiram to come, too.

"Seven o'clock, sharp, remember—and I'll be dreadfully disappointed if you don't come," added Lettie, turning her horse's head homeward, and saying it with so much cordiality that her hearer's heart warmed.

"She is pretty," mused Sister, watching the bay horse and its rider flying along the road. "I don't blame Hiram for thinking she's the very finest girl in these parts.

"She is," declared Sister, emphatically, and shook herself.

Hiram had finished husking the lowland corn that day, with Henry's help, and it was all drawn in at night. When the last measured basket was heaped in the crib by lantern light, the young farmer added up the figures chalked up on the lintel of the door.

"For goodness' sake, Hiram! it isn't as much as that, is it?" gasped Henry, viewing the figures the young farmer wrote proudly in his memorandum book.

"Six acres—six hundred and eighty baskets of sound corn," crowed "Hiram. And it's corn that is corn, as Mr. Bronson says.

"It's not quite as hard as the upland corn, for the growing season was not quite long enough for it; but it's better than the average in the county——"

"Three hundred and forty bushel of shelled corn from six acres?" cried Henry. "I should say it was! It's worth fifty cents now right at the crib—a hundred and seventy dollars. Hiram! that'll make dad let me go to the agricultural college."

"What?" cried Hiram, surprised and pleased. "Have you really got that idea in your head?"

"I been gnawin' on it ever since you talked so last spring," admitted his friend, rather shyly. "I told father, and at first he pooh-poohed.

"But I kept on pointing out to him how much more you knowed than we did—"

"That's nonsense, Henry," interrupted Hiram. "Only about some things. I wouldn't want to set myself up over the farmers of this neighborhood as knowing so much."

"Well, you've proved it. Dad says so himself. He was taken all aback when I showed him how you had beat him on the tomato crop. And I been talking to him about your corn.

"That hit father where he lived," chuckled Henry, "for father's a corn-growing man—and always has been considered so in this county.

"He watched the way you tilled your crop, and he believed so much shallow cultivating was wrong, and said so. But he says you beat him on poor ground; and when I tell him what that lowland figures up, he'll throw up his hands.

"And I'm going to take a course in fertilizers, farm management, and the chemistry of soils," continued Henry.

"Just as you say, I believe we have been planting the wrong crops on the right land! Anyway, I'll find out. I believe we've got a good farm, but we're not getting out of it what we should."

"Well, Henry," admitted Hiram, slowly, "nothing's pleased me so much since I came into this neighborhood, as to hear you say this. You get all you can at the experiment station this winter, and I believe that your father will soon begin to believe that there is something in 'book farming', after all."

If it had not been for the hair-hung sword over them, Mrs. Atterson and Hiram would have taken great delight in the generous crops that had been vouchsafed to them.

"Still, we can't complain," said the old lady, "and for the first time for more'n twenty years I'm going to be really thankful at Thanksgiving time."

"Oh, I believe you!" cried Sister, who heard her. "No boarders."

"Nope," said the old lady, quietly. "You're wrong. For we're going to have boarders on Thanksgiving Day. I've writ to Crawberry. Anybody that's in the old house now that wants to come to eat dinner with us, can come. I'm going to cook the best dinner I ever cooked — and make a milkpail full of gravy."

"I know," said the good old soul, shaking her head, "that them two old maids I sold out to have half starved them boys. We ought to be able to stand even Fred Crackit, and Mr. Peebles, one day in the year."

"Well!" returned Sister, thoughtfully. "If you can stand 'em I can. I never did think I could forgive 'em all — so mean they was to me — and the hair-pulling and all.

"But I guess you're right, Mis' Atterson. It's heapin' coals of fire on their heads, like what the minister at the chapel says."

"Good Land o' Goshen, child!" exclaimed the old lady, briskly. "Hot coals would scotch 'em, and I only want to fill their stomachs for once."

The husking at the Bronsons was a very well attended feast, indeed. There was a great barn floor, and on this were heaped the ear-corn in the husks — not too much, for Lettie proposed having the floor cleared and swept for square dancing, and later for the supper.

She had a lot of her school friends at the husking, and at first the neighborhood boys and girls were bashful in the company of the city girls.

But after they got to work husking the corn, and a few red ears had been found (for which each girl or boy had to pay a forfeit) they became a very hilarious company indeed.

Now, Lettie, broadly hospitable, had invited the young folk far and wide. Even those whom she had not personally seen, were expected to attend.

So it was not surprising that Pete Dickerson should come, despite the fact that Mr. Bronson had once discharged him from his employ — and for serious cause.

But Pete was not a thin-skinned person. Where there was anything "doing" he wanted to cut a figure. And his desire to be important, and be marked by the company, began to make him objectionable before the evening was half over.

For instance, he thought it was funny to take a run down the long barn floor and leap over the heads of those huskers squatting about a heap of corn, and land with his heavy boots on the apex of the pile, thus scattering the ears in all directions.

He got long straws, too, and tickled the backs, of the girls' necks; or he dumped handfuls of bran down their backs, or shook oats into their hair—and the oats stuck.

Mr. Bronson could not see to everything; and Pete was very sly at his tricks. A girl would shriek in one corner, and the lout would quickly transport himself to a distant spot.

When the corn was swept aside, and the floor cleared for the dance, Pete went beyond the limit, however. He had found a pail of soft-soap in the shed and while the crowd was out of the barn, playing a "round game" in the yard while it was being swept, Pete slunk in with the soap and a swab, and managed to spread a good deal of the slippery stuff around on the boards.

A broom would not remove this soft-soap. When the hostler swept, he only spread it. And when the dancing began many a couple measured their length on the planks, to Pete's great delight.

But the hired man had observed Pete sneaking about while he was removing the last of the corn, and Hiram Strong discovered soft-soap on Pete's clothes, and the smell of it strong upon his unwashed hands.

"You get out of here," Mr. Bronson told the boy. "I had occasion to put you off my land once, and don't let me have to do it a third time," and he shoved him with no gentle hand through the door and down the driveway.

But Pete laid it all to Hiram. He called back over his shoulder:

"I'll be square with you, yet, Hi Strong! You wait!"

But Hiram bad been threatened so often from that quarter by now, that he was not much interested.

CHAPTER XXX
ONE SNOWY MIDNIGHT

The fun went on after that with more moderation, and everybody had a pleasant time. That is, so supposed Hiram Strong until, in going out of the barn again to get a breath of cool air after one of the dances, he almost stumbled over a figure hiding in a corner, and crying.

"Why, Sister!" he cried, taking the girl by the shoulders, and turning her about. "What's the matter?"

"Oh, I want to go home, Hi. This isn't any place for me. Let me—me run—run home!" she sobbed.

"I guess not! Who's bothered you? Has that Pete Dickerson come back?"

"No!" sobbed Sister.

"What is it, then?"

"They—they don't want me here. They don't like me."

"Who don't?" demanded Hiram, sternly.

"Those—those girls from St. Beris. I—I tried to dance, and I slipped on some of that horrid soap and—and fell down. And they said I was clumsy. And one said:

"'Oh, all these country girls are like that. I don't see what Let wanted them here for.'

"'So't we could all show off better,' said another, laughing some more.

"And I guess that's right enough," finished Sister. "They don't want me here. Only to make fun of. And I wish I hadn't come."

Hiram was smitten dumb for a moment. He had danced once with Lettie, but the other town girls had given him no opportunity to do so. And it was plain that Lettie's school friends preferred the few boys who had come up from town to any of the farmers' sons who had come to the husking.

"I guess you're right, Sister. They don't want us—much," admitted Hiram, slowly.

"Then let's both go home," said Sister, sadly.

"No. That wouldn't be serving Mr. Bronson—or Lettie—right. We were invited in good faith, I reckon, and the Bronsons haven't done anything to offend us.

"But you and I'll go back there and dance together. You dance with me—or with Henry; and I'll stick to the country girls. If Lettie Bronson's friends from boarding school think they are so much better than us folks out here in the country, let us show them that we can have a good time without them."

"Oh, I'll go back with you, Hiram," cried Sister, gladly, and the young fellow was a bit conscience-stricken as he noted her changed tone and saw the sparkle that came into her eye.

Had he neglected Sister because Lettie Bronson was about? Well! perhaps he had. But he made up for it with the attention he paid to Sister during the remainder of the evening.

They went home early, however, and Hiram felt somewhat grave after the corn husking. Had Lettie Bronson invited the country-bred young folk living about her father's home, to meet her boarding school friends, and the town boys, merely that the latter might be compared with the farmer-folk to their disfavor?

He could not believe that—really. Lettie Bronson might be thoughtless, and a little proud; but she was still a princess to Hiram, and he could not think this evil of her.

But there were too many duties every day for the young farmer to give much thought to such problems. Harvesting was not complete yet, and soon flurries of snow began to drive across the fields and threaten the approach of winter.

Finally the wind came out of the northwest for more than a day, and toward evening the flakes began to fall, faster and faster, thicker and thicker.

"It's going to be a snowy night—a real baby blizzard," declared Hiram, stamping his feet on the porch before coming into the warm kitchen with the milkpail.

"Oh, dear! And I thought you'd go over to Pollock's with me to-night, Hi," said Sister.

"Mabel an' I are goin' to make our Christmas presents together, and she's expecting me."

"Shucks! 'Twon't be fit for a girl to go out if it snows," said Mother Atterson.

But Hiram saw that Sister was much disappointed, and he had tried to be kinder to her since that night of the corn husking.

"What's a little snow?" he demanded, laughing. "Bundle up good, Sister, and I'll go over with you. I want to see Henry, anyway."

"Crazy young'uns," observed Mother Atterson. But she made no real objection. Whatever Hiram said was right, in the old lady's eyes.

They tramped through the snowy fields with a lantern, and found it half-knee deep in some drifts before they arrived at the Pollocks, short as had been the duration of the fall.

But they were welcomed vociferously at the neighbor's; preparations were made for a long evening's fun; for with the snow coming down so steadily there would be little work done out of doors the following day, so the family need not seek their beds early.

The Pollock children had made a good store of nuts, like the squirrels; and there was plenty of corn to pop, and molasses for candy, or corn-balls, and red apples to roast, and sweet cider from the casks in the cellar.

The older girls retired to a corner of the wide hearth with their work-boxes, and Hiram and Henry worked out several problems regarding the latter's eleven-week course at the agricultural college, which would begin the following week; while the young ones played games until they fell fast asleep in odd corners of the big kitchen.

It was nearly midnight, indeed, when Hiram and Sister started home. And it was still snowing, and snowing heavily.

"We'll have to get all the plows out to-morrow morning!" Henry shouted after them from the porch.

And it was no easy matter to wade home through the heavy drifts.

"I never could have done it without you, Hi," declared the girl, when she finally floundered onto the Atterson porch, panting and laughing.

"I'll take a look around the barns before I come in," remarked the careful young farmer.

This was a duty he never neglected, no matter how late he went to bed, nor how tired he was. Half way to the barn he halted. A light was waving wildly by the Dickerson back door.

It was a lantern, and Hiram knew that it was being whirled around and around somebody's head. He thought he heard, too, a shouting through the falling snow.

"Something's wrong over yonder," thought the young farmer.

He hesitated but for a moment. He had never stepped upon the Dickerson place, nor spoken to Sam Dickerson since the trouble about the turkeys. The lantern continued to swing. Eagerly as the snow came down, it could not blind Hiram to the waving light.

"I've got to see about this," he muttered, and started as fast as he could go through the drifts, across the fields.

Soon he heard the voice shouting. It was Sam Dickerson. And he evidently had been shouting to Hiram, seeing his lantern in the distance.

"Help, Strong! Help!" he called.

"What is it, man?" demanded Hiram, climbing the last pair of bars and struggling through the drifts in the dooryard.

"Will you take my horse and go for the doctor? I don't know where Pete is—down to Cale Schell's, I expect."

"What's the matter, Mr. Dickerson?"

"Sarah's fell down the bark stairs—fell backward. Struck her head an' ain't spoke since. Will you go, Mr. Strong?"

"Certainly. Which horse will I take?"

"The bay's saddled-under the shed—get any doctor—I don't care which one. But get him here."

"I will, Mr. Dickerson. Leave it to me," promised Hiram, and ran to the shed at once.

CHAPTER XXXI
"MR. DAMOCLES'S SWORD"

Hiram Strong was not likely to forget that long and arduous night. It was impossible to force the horse out of a walk, for the drifts were in some places to the creature's girth.

He stopped at the house for a minute and roused Mrs. Atterson and Old Lem and sent them over to help the unhappy Dickersons.

He was nearly an hour getting to the crossroads store. There were lights and revelry there. Some of the lingering crowd were snowbound for the night and were making merry with hard cider and provisions which Schell was not loath to sell them.

Pete was one of the number, and Hiram sent him home with the news of his mother's serious hurt.

He forced the horse to take him into town to Dr. Broderick. It was nearly two o'clock when he routed out the doctor, and it was four o'clock when the physician and himself, in a heavy sleigh and behind a pair of mules, reached the Dickerson farmhouse.

The woman had not returned to consciousness, and Mrs. Atterson remained through the day to do what she could. But it was many a tedious week before Mrs. Dickerson was on her feet again, and able to move about.

Meanwhile, more than one kindly act had Mother Atterson done for the neighbors who had seemed so careless of her rights. Pete never appeared when either Mrs. Atterson or Sister came to the house; but in his sour, gloomy way, Sam Dickerson seemed to be grateful.

Hiram kept away, as there was nothing he could do to help them. And he saw when Pete chanced to pass him, that the youth felt no more kindly toward him than he had before.

"Well, let him be as ugly as he wants to be—only let him keep away from the place and let our things alone," thought Hiram. "Goodness knows! I'm not anxious to be counted among Pete Dickerson's particular friends."

Thanksgiving came on apace, and every one of the old boarders of Mother Atterson had written that he would come to the farm to spend the holiday. Even Mr. Peebles acknowledged the invitation with thanks, but adding that he hoped Sister would not forget he must "eschew any viands at all greasy, and that his hot water was to be at 101, exactly."

"The poor ninny!" ejaculated Mother Atterson. "He doesn't know what he wants. Sister only poured it out of the teakettle, and he had to wait for it to cool, anyway, before he could drink it."

But it was determined to give the city folk a good time, and this determination was accomplished. Two of Sister's turkeys, bought and paid for in hard cash by Mother Atterson, graced the long table in the sitting-room.

Many of the good things with which the table was laden came from the farm. And, without Hiram and Sister, and Old Lem Camp, Mrs. Atterson made even Fred Crackit understand, these good things had not been possible!

But the Crawberry folk, as a whole, were much subdued. They had missed Mother Atterson dreadfully; and, really, they had felt some affection for their old landlady, after all.

After dinner Fred Crackit, in a speech that was designed to be humorous, presented a massive silver plated water-pitcher with "Mother Atterson" engraved upon it. And really, the old lady broke down at that.

"Good Land o' Goshen!" she exclaimed. "Why, you boys do think something of the old woman, after all, don't ye?

"I must say that I got ye out here more than anything to show ye what we could do in the country. 'Specially how it had improved Sister. And how Hiram Strong warn't the ninny you seemed to think he was. And that Mr. Camp only needed a chance to be something in the world again.

"Well, well! It wasn't a generous feeling I had toward you, mebbe; but I'm glad you come and—I hope you all had enough gravy."

So the occasion proved a very pleasant one indeed. And it made a happy break in the hard work of preparing for the winter.

The crops were all gathered ere this, and they could make up their books for the season just passed.

But there was wood to get in, for all along they had not had wood enough, and to try and get wood out of the snowy forest in winter for immediate use in the stoves was a task that Hiram did not enjoy.

He had Henry to help him saw a goodly pile before the first snow fell; and Mr. Camp split most of it and he and Sister piled it in the shed.

"We've got to haul up enough logs by March—or earlier—to have a wood sawing in earnest," announced Hiram. "We must get a gasoline engine and saw, and call on the neighbors for help, and have a sawing-bee."

"But what will be the use of that if we've got to leave here in February?" demanded Mrs. Atterson, worriedly. "The last time I saw that Pepper in town he grinned at me in a way that made me want to break my old umbrel' over his dratted head!"

"I don't care," said Hiram, sullenly. "I don't want to sit idle all winter. I'll cut the logs, anyway, and draw 'em out from time to time. If we have to leave, why, we have to, that's all."

"And we can't tell a thing to do about next year till we know what Pepper is going to do," groaned Mrs. Atterson.

"That is very true. But if he doesn't exercise his option before February tenth, we needn't worry any more. And after that will be time enough to make our plans for next season's crops," declared Hiram, trying to speak more cheerfully.

But Mrs. Atterson went around with clouded brow again, and was heard to whisper, more than once, something about "Mr. Damocles's sword."

CHAPTER XXXII
THE CLOUD IS LIFTED

Despite Hiram Strong's warning to his employer when they started work on the old Atterson Eighty, that she must expect no profit for this season's, work, the Christmas-tide, when they settled their accounts for the year, proved the young fellow to have been a bad prophet.

"Why, Hiram, after I pay you this hundred dollars, I shall have a little money left—I shall indeed. And all that corn in the crib—and stacks of fodder, beside the barn loft full, and the roots, and the chickens, and the pork, and the calf——"

"Why, Hiram! I'm a richer woman to-day than when I came out here to the farm, that's sure. How do you account for it?"

Hiram had to admit that they had been favored beyond his expectations.

"If that Pepper man would only come for'ard and say what he was going to do!" sighed Mother Atterson.

That was the continual complaint now. As the winter advanced all four of the family bore the option in mind continually. There was talk of the railroad going before the Legislature to ask for the condemnation of the property it needed, in the spring.

It seemed pretty well settled that the survey along the edge of the Atterson Eighty would be the route selected. And, if that was the case, why did Pepper not try to exercise his option?

Mr. Strickland had said that there was no way by which the real estate man's hand could be forced; so they had to abide Pepper's pleasure.

"If we only knew we'd stay," said Hiram, "I'd cut a few well grown pine trees, while I am cutting the firewood, have them dragged to the mill, and saw the boards we shall need if we go into the celery business this coming season."

"What do you want boards for?" demanded Henry, who chanced to be home over Christmas, and was at the house.

"For bleaching. Saves time, room, and trouble. Banking celery, even with a plow, is not alone old-fashioned, and cumbersome, but is apt to leave the blanched celery much dirtier."

"But you'll need an awful lot of board for six acres, Hiram!" gasped Henry.

"I don't know. I shall run the trenches four feet apart, and you mustn't suppose, Henry, that I shall blanch all six acres at once. The boards can be used over and over again."

"I didn't think of that," admitted his friend.

Henry was eagerly interested in his selected studies at the experiment station and college, and Abel Pollock followed his son's work there with growing approval, too.

"It does beat all," he admitted to Hiram, "what that boy has learned already about practical things. Book-farming ain't all flapdoodle, that's sure!"

So the year ended—quietly, peacefully, and with no little happiness in the Atterson farmhouse, despite the cloud that overshadowed the farm-title, and the doubts which faced them about the next season's work.

They sat up on New Year's eve to see the old year out and the new in, and had a merry evening although there were only the family. When the distant whistles blew at midnight they went out upon the back porch to listen.

It was a dark night, for thick clouds shrouded the stars. Only the unbroken coverlet of snow (it had fallen that morning) aided them to see about the empty fields.

In the far distance was the twinkle of a single light—that in an upper chamber of the Pollock house. Dickersons' was mantled in shadow, and those two houses were the only ones in sight of the Atterson place.

"And I was afraid when we came out here that I'd be dead of loneliness in a month—with no near neighbors," admitted Mother Atterson. "But I've been so busy that I ain't never minded it— —

"What's that light, Hiram?"

Her cry was echoed by Sister. Behind the barn a sudden glow was spreading against the low-hung clouds. It was too far away for one of their out-buildings to be afire; but Hiram set off immediately, although he only had slippers on, for the corner of the barnyard fence.

When he reached this point he saw that one of the fodder stacks in the cornfield was afire. The whole top of the stack was ablaze.

"Oh, dear! Oh, dear!" cried Sister, who had followed him. "What can we do?"

"Nothing,", said Hiram. "There's no wind, and it won't spread to another stack. But that one is past redemption, for sure!"

Hiram hastened back to the house and put on his boots. But he did not wade through the snow to the fodder stack that was burning so briskly. He merely made a detour around it, at some yards distant. Nowhere did he see the mark of a footprint.

How the stack had been set afire was a mystery. Hiram had stacked the fodder himself, with the help of Sister, who had pitched the bundles up to him. The young farmer did not smoke, and he seldom carried matches loose in his pockets.

Therefore, the idea that he had dropped a match in the fodder and a field mouse, burrowing for some nubbin of corn, had come across the match, nibbled the head, and so set the blaze, was scarcely feasible.

Yet, how else had the fire started?

When daylight came Hiram could find no footprint near the stack— only his own where he had circled it while it was blazing.

It was the stack nearest to the Dickerson line. Hiram, naturally, thought of Pete.

Since Mrs. Dickerson's sickness, Mother Atterson had been back and forth to help her neighbor, and whenever Sam Dickerson saw Hiram he was as friendly as it was in the nature of the man to be.

Hiram could not believe that Pete's father would now countenance any of his son's meannesses; yet when the young farmer went along the line fence, he saw fresh tracks across the Dickerson fields, and discovered where the person had stood, on the Dickerson side of the fence opposite the burned fodder stack.

But these footprints were all of three hundred feet from the stack, and there was not a mark in the snow upon Hiram's side of the fence, saving his own footprints.

"Maybe somebody merely ran across to look at the blaze. But it's strange I did not see him," thought Hiram.

He could not help being suspicious, however, and he prowled about the stacks and the barns more than ever at night. He could not shake off the feeling that the enemy in the dark was at work again.

January passed, and the fatal day—the tenth of February—drew nearer and nearer. If Pepper proposed to exercise his option he must do it on or before that date.

Neither Hiram nor Mrs. Atterson had seen the real estate man of late; but they had seen Mr. Strickland, and on the final day they drove to town to meet Pepper—if the man was going to show up—in the lawyer's office.

"I wouldn't trouble him, if I were you," advised the lawyer. "But if you insist, I'll send over for him."

"I want to know what he means by all this," declared Mrs. Atterson, angrily. "He's kept me on tenter-hooks for ten months, and there ought to be some punishment for the crime."

"I am afraid he has been within his rights," said the lawyer, smiling; but he sent his clerk for the real estate man, probably being very well convinced of the outcome of the affair.

In came the snaky Mr. Pepper. The moment he saw Mrs. Atterson and Hiram he began to cackle.

"Ye don't mean to say you come clean in here this stormy day to try and sell that farm to me?" asked the real estate man. "No, ma'am! Not for no sixteen hundred dollars. If you'll take twelve——"

Mrs. Atterson could not find words to reply to him; and Hiram felt like seizing the scoundrel by the scruff of his neck and throwing him down to the street. But it was Mr. Strickland who interposed:

"So you do not propose to exercise your option?"

"No, indeed-y!"

"How long since did you give up the idea of purchasing the Atterson place?" asked the lawyer, curiously.

"Pshaw! I gave up the idee 'way back there last spring," chuckled Pepper.

"You haven't the paper with you, have you, Mr. Pepper?" asked Mr. Strickland, quietly.

The real estate man looked wondrous sly and tapped the side of his nose with a lean finger.

"Why, I tore up that old paper long ago. It warn't no good to me," said Pepper. "I wouldn't take the farm at that price for a gift," and he departed with a sneering smile upon his lips.

"And well he did destroy it," declared Mr. Strickland. "It was a forgery — that is what it was. And if we could have once got Pepper in court with it, he would not have turned another scaly trick for some years to come."

CHAPTER XXXIII
"CELERY MAD"

The relief to the minds of Hiram Strong and Mrs. Atterson was tremendous.

Especially was the young farmer inspired to greater effort. He saw the second growing season before him. And he saw, too, that now, indeed, he had that chance to prove his efficiency which he had desired all the time.

The past year had cost him little for clothing or other expenses. He had banked the hundred dollars Mrs. Atterson had paid him at Christmas.

But he looked forward to something much bigger than the other hundred when the next Christmas-tide should come. Twenty-five per cent of all the profit of the Atterson Eighty during this second year was to be his own.

The moment "Mr. Damocles's sword", as Mother Atterson had called it, was lifted the young farmer jumped into the work.

He had already cut enough wood to last the family a year; now he got Mr. Pollock, with his team of mules, to haul it up to the house, and then sent for the power saw, asked the neighbors to help, and in less than half a day every stick was cut to stove length.

As he had time Hiram split this wood and Lem Camp piled it in the shed. Hiram knocked together some extra cold-frames, too, and bought some second-hand sash.

And he had already dug a pit for a twelve-foot hotbed. Now, a twelve-foot hotbed will start an enormous number of plants.

Hiram did not plan to have quite so much small stuff in the garden this year, however. He knew that he should have less time to work in the garden. He proposed having more potatoes, about as many tomatoes as the year before, but fewer roots to bunch, salads and the like. He must give the bulk of his time to the big commercial crop that he hoped to put into the bottom-land.

He had little fear of the river overflowing its banks late enough in the season to interfere with the celery crop. For the seedlings were to be handled in the cold-frames and garden-patch until it was time to set them in the trenches. And that would not be until July.

He contented himself with having the logs he cut drawn to the sawmill and the sawed planks brought down to the edge of the bottom-land, and did not propose to put a plow into the land until late June.

Meanwhile he started his celery seed in shallow boxes, and when the plants were an inch and a half, or so, tall, he pricked them out, two inches apart each way into the cold-frames.

Sister and Mr. Camp could help in this work, and they soon filled the cold-frames with celery plants destined to be reset in the garden plat later.

This "handling" of celery aids its growth and development in a most wonderful manner. At the second transplanting, Hiram snipped back the tops, and the roots as well, so that each plant would grow sturdily and not be too "stalky".

Mrs. Atterson declared they were all celery mad. "Whatever will you do with so much of the stuff, I haven't the least idee, Hiram. Can you sell it all? Why, it looks to me as though you had set out enough already to glut the Crawberry market."

"And I guess that's right," returned Hiram. "Especially if I shipped it all at once."

But he was aiming higher than the Crawberry market. He had been in correspondence with firms that handled celery exclusively in some of the big cities, and before ever he put the plow into the bottom-land he had arranged for the marketing of every stalk he could grow on his six acres.

It was a truth that the family of transplanted boarding house people worked harder this second spring than they had the first one. But they knew how better, too, and the garden work did not seem so arduous to Sister and Old Lem Camp.

Mrs. Atterson had a fine flock of hens, and they had laid well after the first of December, and the eggs had brought good prices. She planned to increase her flock, build larger yards, and in time make a business of poultry raising, as that would be something that she and Sister could practically handle alone.

Sister's turkeys had thrived so the year before that she had saved two hens and a handsome gobbler, and determined to breed turkeys for the fall market.

And Sister learned a few things before she had raised "that raft of poults," as Mother Atterson called them. Turkeys are certainly calculated to breed patience—especially if one expects to have a flock of young Toms and hens fit for killing at Thanksgiving-time.

She hatched the turkeys under motherly hens belonging to Mother Atterson, striving to breed poults that would not trail so far from the house; but as soon as the youngsters began to feel their wings they had their foster-mothers pretty well worn out. One flock tolled the old hen off at least a mile from the house and Hiram had some work enticing the poults back again.

There was no raid made upon her turkey coops this year, however. Pete Dickerson was not much in evidence during the spring and early summer. Mrs. Atterson went back and forth to the neighbors; but although whenever Hiram saw the farmer the latter put forth an effort to be pleasant to him, the two households did not well "mix".

Besides, during this busiest time of the year, when the crops were getting started, there seemed to be little opportunity for social intercourse. At least, so it seemed on the Atterson place.

They were a busy and well contented crew, and everything seemed to be running like clockwork, when suddenly "another dish of trouble", as Mother Atterson called it, was served them in a most unexpected manner.

Hiram was coming up from the barn one evening, long after dark, and had just caught sight of Sister standing on the porch waiting for him, when a sudden glow against the dark sky, made him turn.

The flash of fire passed on the instant, and Sister called to him:

"Oh, Hiram! did you see that shooting-star?"

"You never wished on it, Sis," said the young farmer.

"Oh, yes I did!" she returned, dancing down the steps to meet him.

"That quick?"

"Just that quick," she reiterated, seizing his arm and getting into step with him.

"And what was the wish?" demanded Hiram.

"Why—I won't ever get it if I tell you, will I?" she queried, shyly.

"Just as likely to as not, Sister," he said, with serious voice. "Wishes are funny things, you know. Sometimes the very best ones never come true."

"And I'm afraid mine will never come true," she sighed. "Oh, dear! I guess no amount of wishing will ever bring some things to pass."

"Maybe that's so, Sis," he said, chuckling. "I fancy that getting out and hustling for the thing you want is the best way to fulfill wishes."

"Oh, but I can't do that in this case," said the girl, shaking her head, and still speaking very seriously as they came to the porch steps.

"Maybe I can bring it about for you," teased Hiram.

"I guess not," she said. "I want so to be like other girls, Hiram! I'd like to be like that pretty Lettie Bronson. I'm not jealous of her looks and her clothes and her good times and all; no, that's not it," proclaimed Sister, with a little break in her voice.

"But I'd like to know who I really be. I want folks, and—and I want to have a real name of my own!"

"Why, bless you!" exclaimed the young fellow, "'Sister' is a nice name, I'm sure—and we all love it here."

"But it isn't a name. They call me Sissy Atterson at school. But it doesn't belong to me. I—I've thought lots about choosing a name for myself—a real fancy one, you know. There's lots of pretty, names," she said, reflectively.

"Cords of 'em," Hiram agreed.

"But, you see, they wouldn't really be mine," said the girl, earnestly. "Not even after I had chosen them. I want my very own name! I want to know who I am and all about myself. And"—with a half strangled sob—"I guess wishing will never bring me that, will it, Hiram?"

Never before had the young fellow heard Sister express herself upon this topic. He had no idea that the girl felt her unknown and practically unnamed existence so strongly.

"I wouldn't care, Sis," he said, patting her bent shoulders. "We love you here just as well as we would if you had ten names! Don't forget that.

"And maybe it won't be all a mystery some day. Your folks may look you up. They may come here and find you. And they'll be mighty proud of you—you've grown so tall and good looking. Of course they will!"

Sister listened to him and gave a little contented sigh. "And then they might want to take me away—and I'd fight, tooth and nail, if they tried it."

"What?" gasped Hiram.

"Of course I would!" said the girl. "Do you suppose I'd give up Mother Atterson for a dozen families—or for clothes—and houses—or, or anything?" and she ran into the house leaving the young farmer in some amazement.

"Ain't that the girl of it?" he muttered, at last. "Yet I bet she is in earnest about wanting to know about her folks."

And from that time Hiram thought more about Sister's problem himself than he had before. Once, when he went to Crawberry, he went to the charitable institution from which Mother Atterson had taken Sister. But the matron had heard nothing of the lawyer who had once come to talk over the child's affairs, and the path of inquiry seemed shut off right there by an impassable barrier.

However, this is ahead of our story. On this particular night Hiram washed at the pump, and then followed Sister in to supper.

Before they were half through Mr. Camp suddenly started from his chair and pointed through the window.

Flames were rising behind the barn again!

"Another stack burning!" exclaimed Hiram, and be shot out of the door, seizing a pail of water, hoping that he might put it out.

But the stack was doomed. He knew it the moment he saw the extent of the blaze.

He kept away from it, as he had before; yet he did not expect to pick up any trail of the incendiary near the stack.

"Twice in the same place is too much!" declared the young farmer, glowing with wrath. "I'm going to have this mystery explained, or know the reason why."

He left Mr. Camp to watch the burning fodder, to see that sparks from the stack did no harm, and lighting his lantern he went along the line fence again.

Yes! there were the footprints that he had expected to find. But the burning stack was even farther from the fence than the first one had been— and there were no marks of feet in the soft earth on Mrs. Atterson's side of the boundary.

CHAPTER XXXIV
CLEANING UP A PROFIT

Hiram crawled through the wires, and followed the plain foot-marks back to the Dickerson sheds. He lost them there, of course, but he knew by the size of the footprints that either Sam Dickerson or his oldest son had been over to the line fence.

"And that shooting-star!" considered Hiram. "There was something peculiar about that. I wonder if there wasn't a shooting star, also, away back there at New Year's when our other stack of fodder was burned?"

He loitered about the sheds for a few moments. It appeared as though all the Dickersons were indoors. Nobody interfered with him.

Of a sudden Hiram began to sniff an odor that seemed strange about a cart-shed. At least, no wise farmer would have naphtha, or gasoline, in his outbuildings, for it would make his insurance invalid.

But that was the smell Hiram discovered. And he was not long in finding the cause of it.

Back in a dark corner, upon a beam, lay a big sling-shot—one of those that boys swing around their heads with a stone in the heel of it, and then let go one end to shoot the missile to a distance.

The leather loop was saturated with the gasoline, and it had been scorched, too. The smell of burning, as well as the smell of gasoline, was very distinct.

Hiram took the sling-shot with him, and went up to the Dickerson house.

He had got along so well with the Dickersons for these past months that he honestly shrank from "starting anything" now. Yet he could not overlook this flagrant piece of malicious mischief. Indeed, it was more than that. Two stacks had already been burned, and it might be some of the outbuildings— or even Mrs. Atterson's house—next time!

Besides, Hiram felt himself responsible for his employer's property. The old lady could not afford to lose the fodder, and Hiram was determined that both of the burned stacks should be paid for in full.

He looked through the window of the Dickerson kitchen. The family was around the supper table-Mr. and Mrs. Dickerson, Pete, and the children, little and big. It was a cheerful family group, after all. Rough and uncouth as the farmer was, Dickerson likely had his feelings like other people. Instead of bursting right in at the door as had been Hiram's intention, and accusing Pete to his face, the indignant young fellow hesitated.

He hadn't any sympathy for Pete, not the slightest. If he gave him—or the elder Dickerson—a chance to clear up matters by making good to Mrs. Atterson for what she had lost, Hiram Strong decided that he was being very lenient indeed.

He stepped quietly onto the porch and rapped on the door. Then he backed off and waited for some response from within.

"Hullo, Mr. Strong!" exclaimed the farmer, coming himself to the "door. Why! is that your stack burning?"

"Yes, sir," said Hiram, quietly.

"Another one!"

"That is the second," admitted Hiram. "But I don't propose that another shall be set afire in just the same way."

Sam Dickerson stepped suddenly down to the young farmer's level, and asked:

"What do you mean by that? Do you know how it got afire?"

Hiram held out the sling-shot in the light of his lantern.

"A rag, saturated with gasoline, was wrapped around a pebble, then set afire, and stone and blazing rag were shot from our line fence into the fodderstack.

"I found the footprints of the incendiary on New Year's morning at the same place. And I'll wager a good deal that your son Pete's boots will fit the footprints over there at the line now!"

Sam Dickerson's face had turned exceedingly red, and then paled. But he spoke very quietly.

"What are you going to do with him, Mr. Strong?" he asked. "It will be five years for him at least, if you take it to court—and maybe longer."

"I don't believe, Mr. Dickerson, that you have upheld Pete in all the mean tricks he has played on me."

"Indeed I haven't! And since I got a look at myself—back there when the wife was hurt——"

Sam Dickerson's voice broke and he turned away for a moment so that his visitor should not see his face.

"Well!" he continued. "You've got Pete right this time—no doubt of that. I dunno what makes him such a mean whelp. I'll lambaste him good for this, now I tell you. But the stacks——"

"Make him pay for them out of his own money. Mrs. Atterson ought not to lose the stacks," said Hiram, slowly.

"Oh, he'll do that, anyway, you can bet!" exclaimed Dickerson, with conviction.

"I don't believe that sending a boy like him to jail will either improve his morals, or do anybody else any good," observed Hiram, reflectively.

"And it'll jest about finish his mother," spoke Sam.

"That's right, too," said the young farmer. "I tell you. I don't want to see him—not just now. But you do what you think is best about this matter, and make Peter pay the bill—ten dollars for the two stacks of fodder."

"He shall do it, Mr. Strong," declared Sam Dickerson, warmly. "And he shall beg your pardon, too, or I'll larrup him until he can't stand. He's too big for a lickin', but he ain't too big for me to lick!"

And the elder Dickerson was as good as his word. An hour later yells from the cart shed denoted that Pete was finally getting what he should have received when he was a younger boy.

Before noon Sam marched the youth over to Mrs. Atterson. Pete was very puffy about the eyes, and his cheeks were streaked with tears. Nor did he seem to care to more than sit upon the extreme edge of a chair.

But he paid Mrs. Atterson ten dollars, and then, nudged by his father, turned to Hiram and begged the young farmer's pardon.

"That's all right, etc.," said Hiram, laying his hand upon the boy's shoulder. "Just because we haven't got on well together heretofore, needn't make any difference between us after this.

"Come over and see me. If you have time this summer and want the work, I'll be glad to hire you to help handle my celery crop.

"Neighbors ought to be neighborly; and it won't do either of us any good to hug to ourselves any injury which we fancy the other has done. We'll be friends if you say so, Peter—though I tell you right now that if you turn another mean trick against me, I'll take the law into my own hands and give you worse than you've got already."

Pete looked sheepish enough, and shook hands. He knew very well that Hiram could do as he promised.

But from that time on the young farmer had no further trouble with him.

Meanwhile Hiram's crops on the Atterson Eighty grew almost as well this second season as they had the first. There was a bad drouth this year, and the upland corn did not do so well; yet the young farmer's corn crop compared well with the crops in the neighborhood.

He had put in but eight acres of corn this year; but they had plenty of old corn in the crib when it came time to take down this second season's crop.

It was upon the celery that Hiram bent all his energies. He had to pay out considerable for help, but that was no more than he expected. Celery takes a deal of handling.

When the long, hot, dry days came, when the uplands parched and the earth fairly seemed to radiate the heat, the acres of tender plants which Hiram and his helpers had just set out in the trenches began to wilt most discouragingly.

Henry Pollock, who did all he could to aid Hiram on the crop, shook his head in despair.

"It's a-layin' down on you, Hiram—it's a-layin' down on you. Another day like this and your celery crop will be pretty small pertaters!"

"And that would be a transformation worthy of the attention of all the agricultural schools, Henry," returned the young farmer, grimly laughing.

"You got a heart—to laugh at your own loss," said Henry.

"There isn't any loss—yet," declared Hiram.

"But there's bound to be," said his friend, a regular "Job's comforter" for the nonce.

"Look here, Henry; you'd have me give up too easy. 'Never say die!' That's the farmer's motto."

"Jinks!" exclaimed young Pollock, "they're dying all around us just the same—and their crops, too. We ain't going to have half a corn crop if this spell of dry weather keeps on. And the papers don't give us a sign of hope."

"When there doesn't seem to be a sign of hope is when the really up-to-date farmer begins to actually work," chuckled Hiram.

"And just tell me what you're going to do for this field of wilted celery?" demanded Henry.

"Come on up to the house and I'll get Mother Atterson to give us an early supper," quoth Hiram. "I'm going to town and I invite you to go with me."

Henry had got used by this time to Hiram's little mysteries. But this seemed to him a case where man had done all that could be done for the crop, and without Providential interposition, "the whole field would have to go to pot", as he expressed it.

And in his heart the young farmer knew that the outlook for a paying crop of celery right then was very small indeed. He had done his best in preparing the soil, in enriching it, in raising the sets and transplanting them—up to this point he had brought his big commercial crop, at considerable expense. If the drouth really "got" it, he would have, at the most, but a poor and stunted crop to ship in the Fall.

But Hiram Strong was not the fellow to throw up his hands and own himself beaten at such a time as this. Here was an obstacle that must be overcome. The harder the problem looked the more determined he was to solve it.

The two boys drove to town that evening and Hiram sought out a man who contracted to move houses, clean cisterns and wells, and various work of that kind. He knew this man had just the thing he needed, and after a conference with him, Hiram loaded some bulky paraphernalia into the light wagon—it was so dark Henry could not see what it was—and they drove home again.

"I'd like to know what the Jim Hickey you're about, Hiram," sniffed Henry, in disgust. "What's all this litter back here in the wagon?"

"You come over and give me a hand in the morning—early now, say by sun-up—and you'll find out. I want a couple of husky chaps like you," chuckled Hiram. "I'll get Pete Dickerson to work against me."

"If you do, you tell Pete he'll have to work lively," said Henry, with a grin. "I don't know what it is you want us to do, but I reckon I can keep my end up with Pete, from hoein' 'taters to cuttin' cord-wood."

"You can keep your end up with him, can you?" chuckled Hiram. "Well! I bet you can't in this game I'm going to put you two fellows up against."

"What! Pete Dickerson beat me at anything—unless it's sleeping?" grunted Henry, with vast disgust. "I'll keep my end up with him at anything."

And the more assured he was of this the more Hiram was amused. "Come on over early, Henry," said the young farmer, "and I'll show you that there's at least one thing in which you can't keep your end up with Pete."

His friend was almost angry when he started off across the fields for home; but he was mighty curious, too. That curiosity, if nothing more, would have brought him to the Atterson house in good season the following morning.

Already, however, Hiram and Pete—with the light wagon—had gone down to the riverside. Henry hurried after them and reached the celery field just as the red face of the sun appeared.

There had been little dew during the night and the tender transplants had scarcely lifted their heads. Indeed, the last acre set out the day before were flat.

On the bank of the river, and near that suffering acre, were Hiram and Pete Dickerson. Henry hurried to them, wondering at the thing he saw upon the bank.

Hiram was already laying out between the celery rows a long hosepipe. This was attached to a good-sized force-pump, the feedpipe of which was in the river. It was a two-man pump and was worked by an up-and-down "brake."

"Catch hold here, Henry," laughed Hiram. "One of you on each side now, and pump for all you're worth. And see if I'm not right, my boy. You can't keep your end up with Pete at this job; for if you do, the water won't flow!"

Henry admitted that he had, been badly sold by the joke; but he was enthusiastic in his praise of Hiram's ingenuity, too.

"Aw, say!" said the young farmer, "what do you suppose the Good Lord gave us brains for? Just so as to keep our fingers out of the fire? No, sir! With all this perfectly good and wet water running past my field, could I have the heart to let this celery die? I guess not!"

He had a fine spray nozzle on the pipe and the pipe itself was long enough so that, by moving the pump occasionally, he could water every square foot of the big piece. And the three young fellows, by changing about, went over the field every other day in about four hours without difficulty.

By and by the celery plants got rooted well; they no longer drooped in the morning; before the drouth was past the young farmer had as handsome a field of celery as one would wish. Indeed, when he began to ship the crop, even his earliest crates were rated A-1 by the produce men, and he bad no difficulty in selling the entire crop at the top of the market, right through the season.

The garden paid a profit; the potatoes did even better than the year before, and Hiram harvested and sold seventy-five dollars' worth while the price for new potatoes was high.

He shipped most of his tomatoes this year, for he could not pay attention to the local market as he had the first season; but the tomato crop was a good one.

They raised to eight weeks and sold, during the year, five pair of shoats, and Mrs. Atterson bought a grade cow with her calf by her side, for a hundred dollars, and made ten pounds of butter a week right through the season.

Old Lem Camp, looking ten years younger than when he came to the farm, muscular and brown, did all the work about the barns now, milked the cows, and relieved Hiram of all the chores.

Indeed, with some little help about the plowing and cultivating, Hiram knew very well that Mrs. Atterson and Old Lem could run the farm another year without his help.

Of course, the old lady could not expect to put in any crop that would pay her like the celery; for when they footed up their books, the bottom-land had yielded, as Hiram had once prophesied to Mr. Bronson over four hundred dollars the acre, net.

Twenty-four hundred dollars income from six acres; and the profit was more than fifty per cent. Indeed, Hiram's share of the profit amounted to three hundred and seventy dollars.

With his hundred dollar wage, and the money he had saved the previous season, when the crops were harvested this second season, the young farmer's bank book showed a balance of over five hundred dollars to his credit.

"I'm eighteen years old and over," soliloquized the young farmer. "And I've got a capital of five hundred dollars. Can't I turn that capital some way go as to give me a bigger—a broader—chance?

"Thus far I've been a one-horse farmer; I want to be something better than that. Now, there's no use in my hanging around here, waiting for something to turn up. I must get a move on me and turn something up for myself."

CHAPTER XXXV
LOOKING AHEAD

During this year Hiram had not seen much of Mr. Bronson, or Lettie. They had gone back to the West over the summer vacation, and when Lettie had returned for her last year at St. Beris, her father had not come on until near Thanksgiving.

Hiram had spoken with Lettie several times during the fail, and he thought that she had vastly improved in one way, at least.

She could not be any prettier, it seemed to him; but her manner was more cordial, and she always asked after Sister and Mrs. Atterson, and showed that her interest in him was not a mere surface interest.

One day, when Hiram had been shipping some of the last of his celery, Lettie met him on the street near the Scoville railroad station. Hiram was in his high boots, and overalls; and Lettie was with two of her girl friends.

But the girl stopped him and shook hands, and told him that her father had arrived and wanted to see him.

"We want you to come to dinner Saturday evening, Hiram. Father insists, and I shall be very much disappointed if you do not come."

"Why, that's very kind of you, Miss Lettie," responded the young farmer, slowly, trying to find some good reason for refusing the invitation. He was determined not to be patronized.

"Now, Hiram! This is very important. We want you to meet somebody," said Lettie, her eyes dancing. "Somebody very particular. Now! do say you'll come like a good boy, and not keep me teasing."

"Well, I'll come, Miss Lettie," he finally agreed, and she gave him a most charming smile.

Lettie's two friends had waited for her, very much amused.

"I declare, Let!" cried one of them—and her voice reached Hiram's ears quite plainly. "You do have the queerest friends. Why did you stop to speak to that yokel?"

"Hush! he'll hear you," said Miss Bronson; yet she smiled, too. "So you think Hiram is a yokel, do you?"

"Hiram!" repeated her friend. "Goodness me! I should think the name was enough. And those boots—and overalls!"

"Well," said Lettie, still amused, "I've seen my own father in just such a costume. And you know very well that he is a pretty good looking man, dressed up."

"But Let! your father's never a farmer$" gasped the other girl.

"Why not?"

"Oh, she's just joking us," laughed the third girl. "Of course he's a farmer—he owns half a dozen farms. But he's the kind of a farmer who rides around in his automobile and looks over his crops."

"Well, and this young man may do that—in time," said Lettie. "At least, my father believes Hi is aimed that way."

"Nonsense!"

"He doesn't look as though he had a cent," said the third girl.

"He is putting away more money of his very own in the bank than any boy we know, who works. Father says so," declared Lettie. "He says Hi has done wonderfully well with his crops this year—and he is only raising them on shares.

"Let me tell you, girls, the farmer is coming into his own, these days. That is a great saying of father's. He believes that the man who produces the food-stuffs for the rest of the world should have a satisfactory share of the proceeds of their sale. And that is coming, father says.

"Farmers don't have to half starve, and be burdened by mortgages and ignorance, any longer. The country sections are waking up. With good schools and good roads, and the grange, and all, many rural districts are already ahead of the cities in the things worth while."

"Listen to Let lecture!" sniffed one of her friends.

"All right. You wait. Maybe you'll see that same young fellow—Hi Strong—come through this town in his own auto before you graduate from St. Beris."

"Pshaw!" exclaimed the other. "If I do I'll ask him for a ride," and the discussion ended in a laugh.

Perhaps, however, had Hiram heard all Lettie had said he would not have been so doubtful in regard to fulfilling his promise about taking dinner with Mr. Bronson and his daughter on Saturday evening.

To tell the truth, the more he thought of it, the more he shrank from the ordeal. Once he had hoped Mr. Bronson would be the one to show him the way out of the backwater of Crawberry. Hiram had not forgotten how terribly disappointed he had been when he could not find the gentleman's card in the sewer excavation.

And later, when Mr. Bronson had suggested that he leave Mrs. Atterson and come to him to work, Hiram feared that he had missed an opportunity that would never be offered him again. His contract was practically over with his present employer, and Hiram's ambition urged him to desire greater things in the farming line.

It might be in Mr. Bronson's power to aid the young farmer right along this line. The gentleman owned farms in the Middle West that were being tilled on up-to-date methods, and by modern machinery. Hiram desired very strongly to get upon a place of that character. He wished to learn how to handle tools and machinery which it would never pay a "one-horse farmer" to own. But how deeply had the gentleman been offended by Hiram's refusal to come to work for him when he gave him that opportunity? That was a question that bit deep into the young farmer's mind.

When he went to the Bronson's house on Saturday, in good season, Mr. Bronson met him cordially, in the library.

"Well, my boy, they all tell me you have done it!" exclaimed the Westerner.

"Done what?" queried Hiram.

"Made the most money per acre for Mrs. Atterson that this county ever saw. Is that right?"

"I've succeeded in what I set out to do," said Hiram, modestly.

"And I did not believe myself that you could do it," declared the gentleman. "And it's too bad, too, that I was a Doubting Thomas," added Mr. Bronson, his eyes beginning to dance a good deal like Lettie's.

"You see, Hiram, I had it in my mind when I took this place to get a young men from around here and teach him something of my ways of work, and finally take him back West with me.

"I have several farms that are paying me good incomes; but good farm-managers are hard to get. I wanted to train one—a young man. I ran against a promising lad before you came to the Atterson place; but I lost track of him.

"Had you been willing to leave Mrs. Atterson and come to me," continued Mr. Bronson, "I believe I could have licked you into shape last season so that you would have suited me very well," and he laughed outright.

"But now I want you to meet my future farm-manager. He is the very fellow I wanted before I offered the chance to you. I reckon you'll be glad to see him — —"

While he was talking, Mr. Bronson had put his hand on Hiram's shoulder, and urged him down the length of the room. They had come to a heavy portiere; Hiram thought it masked a doorway.

"Here is the fellow himself," exclaimed Bronson suddenly.

The curtain was whisked away. Hiram heard Lettie giggling somewhere in the folds of it. And he found himself staring straight into a long mirror which reflected both himself and the laughing Mr. Bronson.

"Hiram Strong!" spoke the Westerner, admonishingly, "why didn't you tell me long ago that you were the lad who turned my horses out of the ditch that evening back in Crawberry?"

"Why — why — —"

"His fatal modesty," laughed Lettie, appearing and clapping her hands.

"I guess it wasn't that," said Hiram, slowly. "What was the use? I would have been glad of your assistance at the time; but when I found you I had already made a contract with Mrs. Atterson, and — what was the use?"

"Well, perhaps it would have made no difference. When I had dug up the fact that you were the same fellow whom I had looked for at Dwight's Emporium, it struck me that possibly the character that old scoundrel gave you had some basis in fact.

"So I said nothing to you after you had refused to break your contract. That, Hiram, was a good point in your favor. And what that little girl at your house has told Lettie about you — and the way Mrs. Atterson speaks of you, and all — long since convinced me that you were just the lad I wanted.

"Now, Hiram, I believe you know a good deal about farming that I don't know myself. And, at any rate, if you can do what you have done with a run-down place like the Atterson Eighty, I'd like to see what you can do with a bigger and better farm.

"What do you say? Will you come to me — if only for a year? I'll make it worth your while."

And that Hiram Strong did not let this opportunity slip past him will be shown in the next volume of this series, entitled: "Hiram in the Middle West; Or, A Young Farmer's Upward Struggle."

He was sorry to leave Mrs. Atterson at Christmas time; but the old lady saw that it was to Hiram's advantage to go.

"And good land o' Goshen, Hiram! I wouldn't stand in no boy's way — not a boy like you, leastways. You've always been square with me, and you've given me a new lease of life. For I never would have dared to give up the boarding house and come to the farm if it hadn't been for you.

"This is your home — jest as much as it is Sister's home, and Old Lem Camp's. Don't forgit that, Hiram.

"You'll find us all here whenever you want to come back to it. For I've talked with Mr. Strickland and I'm going to adopt Sister, all reg'lar, and she shall have what I leave when I die, only promising to give Mr. Camp a shelter, if he should outlast me.

"Sister's folks may never look her up, and she may never git that money the institution folk think is coming to her. But she'll be well fixed here, that's sure."

Indeed, taking it all around, everybody of importance to the story seemed to be "well fixed", as Mother Atterson expressed it. She herself need never be disturbed by the vagaries of boarders, or troubled in her mind, either waking or sleeping, about the gravy — save on Thanksgiving Day.

Old Lem Camp and Sister were provided for by their own exertions and Mrs. Atterson's kindness. The Dickersons — even Pete — had become friendly neighbors. Henry Pollock had waked up his father, and they were running the Pollock farm on much more modern lines than before.

And Hiram himself was looking ahead to a scheme of life that suited him, and to a chance "to make good" on a much larger scale than he had on the Atterson Eighty where, nevertheless, he had made the soil pay.